T0204795

THE SUFFERINGS OF PRINCE STERNENHOCH

Ladislav Klíma

The Sufferings of Prince Sternenhoch

A GROTESQUE TALE OF HORROR

translated from the Czech by Carleton Bulkin

TWISTED SPOON PRESS
PRAGUE · 2008

ISBN 978-80-86264-33-2

CONTENTS

THE SUFFERINGS OF PRINCE STERNENHOCH

FOREWORD

From the effects of Prince Sternenhoch, one of the foremost magnates of the German Empire at the beginning of this century, who certainly would have become Bismarck's successor as Chancellor if Fate had not thrown the powerful person of Helga-Daemoness onto his path, we have come into possession of a part of his diary. We do not hesitate to make it public, for the story it tells is one of the most terrible and, at the same time, comic of any we know.

We give the events up to August 19, 1912 only in their main outlines, as a brief rendition, not in diary form: as they are only a prologue to the real story. But we have allowed ourselves considerable license elsewhere as well. Mainly, we have somewhat intellectualized our gallant hero. It was necessary. His Excellency was rather inept with a pen . . . At any rate, if the reader wishes to form an impression of what kind of person the prince was and what his handwriting looked like, let him read pp. 161, 162, 190: our hero was not a hair better than his brother, the general. Since the least offense against empirical reality necessarily leads to many others, we have taken the liberty, *but only inasmuch as it concerns the prince's intelligence,* to proceed quite laxly and instinctively, meddlesomely and foolishly, arbitrarily and grandiosely. And we are convinced that by this the heart of the matter not only does not suffer, but gains. What do a few somersaults, paradoxes, errors, absurdities matter? The world itself is a somersault and a paradox, an error and an absurdity. For an author fearful of slip-ups is like someone who has fallen headlong into a cesspool being afraid of getting a little dirty.

And now we present the reader the following amalgam, without further unnecessary apologies, convinced that, as Goethe says of Werther, "neither admiration for the spirit of our hero nor tears for his fate shall be withheld."

I

I first laid eyes on Helga at a certain ball; I was 33, she was 17
years old. My first impression was that this was a downright ugly
girl. A spindly figure, so slender you were frightened of it; a face
disgracefully pale, almost white, terribly thin; a Jewish nose; all
her features, otherwise not bad, somehow withered, somnolent,
hypnotic; she looked like a corpse animated by some mechanism
— and just like her face, even her movements were terribly sluggish and feeble. She had eyes that were constantly downcast like
a bashful little five-year-old girl. Better yet, she had bulky hair,
black as soot . . . I was absolutely ill when my glance first fell
upon her; and when Count M., a dabbler in painting, said: "That
young lady has the most intéressante, classically beautiful face,"
— I could not hold back a laugh. I have no idea how all those
artists and people of "refined taste" can have no taste at all —
evidently they have refined it until there is nothing left of it; whatever I like, they go out of their way not to like, and whatever I

dislike, they like as if on purpose. For example, I wouldn't give the chubby face of any girl from Berlin for the heads of all the Greek stone goddesses, and almost every infantry soldier is better-looking to me than any big-nosed Schiller or Goethe, about whose handsomeness people jaw so much.

But in spite of this, would you believe it? I had to look at her again and again . . . And once, when dancing closely beside me, she happened to lift her eyes while not even looking at me, it was as if she sent a full electric charge through me . . .

And since that day I had to think of her quite often. For whole months. At last I started to forget, then I caught sight of her again; at another aristocrats' ball.

I was most strangely agitated; I could hear the beating of my heart. For a long time I felt as if I were on pins and needles — until finally I asked her for a dance. I made mental excuses to myself: "This from me, the foremost aristocrat of Germany, the owner of 500 million marks, the first advisor and favorite of Wilhelm, an act of magnanimity, noblesse, and grand courtoisie, to offer a dance to the descendant of a family, distinguished centuries ago, now obscure, impoverished, nearly beggarly," as I informed myself directly; "almost no one dances with her, everyone shall praise my deed — and she — how happy she will be!"

But she did not display the least happiness. She stood up mechanically, danced like a wooden doll. Rather unusually confused, I spoke little and stupidly. I don't know what it was from that bony body that penetrated me so narcotically. She didn't lift her eyes once during the whole dance and uttered only two, three words in a gray, almost raspy voice. When the dance was over, I pressed her to myself more firmly and made some kind of mildly lewd witticism. She lightly pushed me away, lifted her eyes. And now they were no longer covered by her upper eyelids — they opened suddenly, unbelievably, until they were like a cat's eyes — just as green, just as wild, predatory, uncanny. Her lips, previously lying sluggishly one on top of the other or slightly parted, closed tightly, became sharp as a razor, her nose became narrow, her nostrils distended and undulated wildly . . . It lasted no longer than a flash of lightning; then she left without a word — a fury again become a corpse — to her old, quite shabby-looking chaperone. I think in that moment I was just as pale as she. What were these sensations fluttering through me? Were they not the mystical apprehension of a horrible future? . . . I tell you: never before had I seen a face even remotely so frightening and eerie, and never would I have believed a face so cadaverously inexpressive, such as I had not seen before or afterward, could become enflamed, like a bolt of lightning from a dark cloud.

It had been decided. A week later I went to her father to ask for her hand — — —

Why did I do so? I don't know: the only thing I know is that it wasn't out of reason.

I did not love her, if love is something beautiful and sweet. However, if what I felt did have something of that emotion, my revulsion toward her was ten times stronger. One thing was certain, that I had loved a dozen women more and it had never occurred to me to accompany one to the altar. And yet something attracted me to her, something dark, something queer, demonic . . . Yes, the devil was in it, and no one else! He so enticed me that at times she seemed to me like a ridiculously legendary gem, the owner of which would be considered a lucky man; that finally, unbelievably! her thinness and pallor sometimes seemed positively exciting to me! Great is the devil's power . . .

And then — I am very susceptible to eccentricities. The thought that I would make her, poor as a church mouse but the offspring of an old and renowned family, out of the clear blue sky, without closer acquaintance, my wife, flattered my vanity. What a sensation it would produce everywhere! I would appear to people as lightning — and selfless, magnanimous, idealistic. And what would His Majesty say to this! And what happiness I would bring to her poor father! Not to mention to her! I had already found out earlier that she was having a very bad time of it with her father; she would certainly worship me as her savior. — I could so easily have married an enormously wealthy girl; but do my 500 million need augmenting? Marry the daughter of an American billionaire who came into his money by selling hogs? I don't doubt that I would have even gotten a princess from a royal family, graceful, endowed with all the right qualities. Well, leaving aside my family and wealth, I may boldly say of myself that I am a beau, in spite of certain faults, for example, that I am only 150 centimeters tall and weigh 45 kilograms, that I am almost toothless, hairless, and whiskerless, also a little squint-eyed and have a noticeable hobble; but even the sun has spots.

I went to her father, a 60-year-old, retired first lieutenant; he couldn't get any higher than that, and had been made to retire a long time ago, not because he was lacking in bravery, intelligence, or dedication, but there wasn't a man alive whom he could stand.

In his milieu he was famous for his strangeness and eccentricity. Oh, how I looked forward to the impression this marvelous offer would make on him! In spite of this my heart was beating with agitation when I knocked on his door.

They lived in two tiny rooms in a garret. Helga was not at home; I heaved a sigh of relief, for at that time I was, I don't know why, terribly afraid of her. The old man lay on the floor, with some kind of box under his head; barefoot, in an undershirt, he was smoking a pipe and spitting at the wall. He left me standing for a while, not replying to my greeting and not looking at me; then he suddenly bounded up so violently that I shrieked and ran for the door, thinking he wanted to strangle me . . . Though even his face alone was capable of frightening one: so strange, wild, and yet somehow boyish; deranged, and yet there was something impressive in it. His eyes, black as lumps of coal, burned like embers of coal. They reminded me of his daughter's eyes when she lifted them to me before, but otherwise there was no similarity between him and her at all.

I introduced myself to him. He took me by the shoulder, stared into my eyes for what seemed like ages, then without a word pulled me into a chair. I was startled, but not offended: I interpreted this severity and crudeness as an expression of unbounded happiness from such a grand visit. And suddenly, without any introduction, as I had resolved to, I said, having gathered my courage: "Permit me, sir, to ask you for the hand of Miss Helga."

But what happened then? Hardly had I uttered these words when everything in my eyes and my soul went dark; I felt as if I had crossed the threshold of the gates of hell, above which is written: "Abandon all hope, ye who enter here . . ."

He was silent for a minute, and not a single muscle moved in his face. Then he growled:

"If you're really Sternenhoch, the bitch is yours. If you're not, you'll be thrown out the door! Prove you are who you say you are!"

Only now did I feel offended and was about to get up either to leave or give this churl a slap in the face. But I didn't do the former, sensing how such sudden proposals would have made me a laughingstock, nor the latter, because I was a little afraid of the lunatic. I threw my calling card on the table.

"Hmm," he growled, "this isn't really a regular identification, but you won't be thrown out the door for now. So you're Willy's main advisor and favorite? Well — you look the part, no doubt of that, you identify yourself better by your face than by that scrap of paper. So when will you tie the knot?"

"That depends on our mutual agreement," I stammered out, not knowing at all what I should think.

"The sooner I have that spook off my hands the better."

"Ugh!" I finally found the energy to say, "Is that any way for a father to speak of his own blood?"

The old man broke into laughter — slapped me on both shoulders in such a way it was a wonder I didn't roll off the chair.

"Because you're such a dupe that you want to become her husband and my son-in-law, I want to tell you a little story. Consider my own blood to be a nasty monster? The devil knows what kind of dolt or turtle or swamp thing jumped my old lady."

"Ugh, ugh, ugh!"

"What a spindly, mute, white spook that one was. For whole nights she would walk back and forth through the rooms — tap, tap, tap . . . Even today, 10 years after she met her end, she still comes to my bed at midnight and whispers: 'Love Helga, look after her, you don't know what you have.' But I fix my eyes on her, fire a pistol at her, and she dissipates like steam. I wanted to have, as is fitting, a son, a real man or, you can't be too choosy, at least a girl with some genuine spark; and there you go! only this miscarriage that a witch stuck me with, who's the biggest rotten stinker I've ever seen, as if on purpose! Can that be my daughter, mine? . . . Well — when she was little she was different — she was so wild that sometimes it was a little much even for me. But I never punished her for it, I praised her; the authorities even called me in a couple of times on her account. I gave her a proper thrashing only once, when she was 10, but not so much to punish her as because I just felt like it. And from that day on she changed completely. All her joy and spirit gone! She stopped speaking and nearly stopped eating. She hung her head — a weeping willow, she wasted away, more and more as time went on. Before, I think she loved me, and having been disappointed in me, she was somehow disappointed in the whole world; so what, because of something so stupid! I didn't touch her for years, hoping it would pass — but no! it only got worse. Then I thought to myself: maybe what got you into this'll also get you out, as is usually the case with madmen or deaf-mutes! — and from that time on I've thrashed her every single day. It's all no use, she keeps shrivelling up, maybe she's gone soft in the head and is getting softer. You can't make something out of nothing; she doesn't give two hoots about anything, as if she were somehow lost, a lost soul that doesn't belong to this world. Perhaps just one time only, praise God, she seemed to recall her old self: I was watching her one night as she stole to my bed with a knife; when she saw that my eyes were open and looking at her calmly, she turned around and walked back into the other room as if nothing had happened. I jumped up and ran after her — she was lying down and sleeping. She gave me no sign the next day that anything had happened, and so to this day I don't know if she really wanted to do me in or if she was sleepwalking, or if it was a phantom of mine or just a dream . . . — That's the way it is, my idiotic little prince. Do you still want her?"

"First of all, don't touch me!" I thundered fearfully, and that out of sheer revulsion, although what I had heard made me reel with horror, and I exclaimed, "And I do! She is certainly a worthy being if one such as you finds her bad, you brute, who have led her to this state by inhuman torment! Shame on you!"

"What a plucky little pipsqueak! But you'll be the right man for her. Ha ha! Only careful, careful — who knows how she'll turn out; perhaps she'll be a mythical dragon, or a walking corpse — maybe it will be intéressante . . . Well, so I can finally be rid of you, go on and run to the priest right away, run, run!"

And he shoved me out the door. And I — to this day I am ashamed — I inquired quite humbly:

"And what am I to make of the fact that, although you long to be rid of your daughter, you treat her suitor in such a way that I am altogether inclined to forget the whole thing, if only to avoid the pleasure of having such an agreeable father-in-law?"

"What should you make of it? That nothing on earth, not even constantly looking at that carcass, could induce me not to treat a rag, a knave, a ragged knave, as is good and proper!"

But this time I really became enraged. "Look here, you!" I roared with unexpected courage, "is this how you speak to the foremost man of the Empire? Just you wait! First thing tomorrow your pension shall be taken from you, you'll be locked up and flogged in the jailhouse by the police until you turn black! And I shall no longer spare a thought for the hand of your daughter!"

And I dashed outside, agitated, but darkly happy that the whole crazy affair had been laid to rest. But hardly had I reached the steps when he ran up behind me and, with terrifying strength, pulled me back inside. Frightened, fearing for the worst, I didn't even put up any resistance to this obvious madman. But he was like a different person now, and he wailed:

"Oh, Your Excellency, do not deign to be angry, ever since you pleased to enter my home I have been a bundle of nerves and my spirit has grown dark. A thousand devils!" he roared, striking his mouth with his fist — but he quickly resumed his wailing: "I esteem Your Excellency most highly, the grandeur of your spirit illuminates your face — ugh! I am boundlessly happy that you have made me, a beggar, a worm unworthy to look upon you, such a wonderful offer! Kindly excuse me!"

"Yes, yes, yes," I panted, half appeased, half afraid that any recalcitrance on my part could provoke a wild outburst of madness.

"You do insist on your offer, don't you?" he implored, with clenched hands.

"Yes, yes — why wouldn't I — it will of course depend on your behavior — "

"Oh, that will be just splendid! I am so happy, Excellency!"

"But what if Helga does not love me?" I said, only in order to say something, trying to wrench my hands from the grip of his fists, which had caught me again.

"Then she will love others, you may set your mind at ease — — but what am I saying, I am an unlucky man, those nerves again . . . What woman wouldn't love you?"

"But what if she simply does not agree?"

"Then I'll whip some sense into her."

"Ugh! Do you think I would want a woman who had been forced to marry me?"

"Of course not! But she will certainly love you, how could she not! There will be no need for the whip, I promise you! If it please Your Excellency to preserve your good favor toward us — well, it would be just splendid good fortune for the bi . . . for her! In the highest social circles she will lose her silliness, among boobs like you she'll be able to make out quite well — but pardon, pardon!"

"Enough!" I said quickly. "Discuss it with her and inform me of her answer in writing! Adieu!"

I was escorted out by his deepest bows. Hardly had the door closed behind me when there came the sound of someone loudly spitting. For the first few moments I was in a chaotic state, but immediately afterward there arose in me the firmest conviction that I would forget the whole affair. This filled me with delight, although at the same time I was burning with shame at all of my crazy, hussar-like bravado. But miserable fate wished that on the street, a few steps from the house, I would run into Helga and that she would look at me with her eyes wide open, enormous, terrible, indescribable. It's a wonder that my combined fright and mysterious terror didn't knock me down; I trembled with cold, my sight grew dark, I didn't even greet her . . .

That meeting was decisive. The devil's snare tightened over me unbreakably. Resistance was no longer possible. Satanic eyes haunted me day and night; I felt they would drive me mad if I didn't deprive them of their power by calling them my own. I vacillated for another week, but it was clear to me how ridiculous, how hopeless it all was.

I replied to the old man's very humble letter, which reached me the very next day after my visit, indicating that Helga agreed without reservation — I replied — —

A month later she was my wife.

·

She went to the altar like a sacrificial lamb; on our wedding night she behaved rather like a puppet that some little girls were playing with — — and I, like an idiot I . . . I don't want to, I cannot, I must not describe it — —

The next morning, when I remembered everything, I felt like taking my own life from shame at what I had done . . . "Perhaps she will change now that she is married, as often happens with women," I said to myself. But now, on the contrary, she was becoming even more listless, corpselike, revolting . . . She never spoke unless asked a question; when asked, she answered, but only on occasion, monosyllabically. No turtle crawls slower than she; no one met her gaze. Naturally she didn't order the servants about. She went around dressed like a ragwoman. She took part in entertainments only when I ordered her to; yet on those occasions she obeyed better than any clock. But her appearance! . . .

"My dear Sternenhoch," Willy told me, "you're acting like Prince Stavrogin, who married a humpbacked, half-witted woman in order to cause a furore, as I read in some silly novel by Dostoevsky." "My dear little boozer," the crown prince spoke to me, "didn't you take that wooden female automaton for a wife, that — what's her name — je m'en fiche, from *The Tales of Hoffmann?*" But one famous poet, whom Willy once granted an audience and who was immediately dispatched with a kick in the ass, told me enthusiastically: "Too often people confuse sleeping and waking, divine repose and laziness, a slowly creeping tiger and a swine. She sleeps and sleeps and sleeps! And her awakening shall be terrible, especially for you, Herr Prince."

And he was right, that poetically-minded sluggard.

Our very first wedding night had its consequences . . . — I point out that I would rather have died, of disgust and of fear and of something else unknown . . . than that a second time I should have — — During her advanced pregnancy I observed marked mental changes in her . . . her eyes were no longer downcast but stared glassily straight ahead, into the mysterious unknown. Her gait grew faster and faster, her voice more clipped and metallic. Whereas she used to stand at the window like a statue for days, or lie on the floor like her estimable papa, now she took long walks outdoors; there were times when she spent whole nights

alone in the forest. She read incessantly. A couple of times, wonder of wonders! she even laughed; she addressed me more often
and would engage in a moment's conversation as normal people
do — —

After her confinement — having borne me a lively little boy
who resembled me — this state of hers soon grew more vigor-
ous and conspicuous. Now she ordered the servants around plenty,
and in such a way that the entire staff submitted to her humbly.
She was always busy writing something. At moments her eyes
would burn with a sinister light, but her usual mood was deeply
pensive, melancholic. And I began to feel toward her, for the first
time in fact, a kind of warmth and desire . . . Once I resolved to
lie down in her bed before she came into her room. Unperturbed,
emotionless, she stared at me at length — and then left for the
kennels, where she spent the entire night in the straw. I trembled
with a disquieting suspicion that there would soon be some unfore-
seeable calamity. — And there was! But the explosion was more
frightening than anything my fantasy had painted.

I sat down overlooking the cradle of my poor son. Helga was
lying some distance away on the divan and writing. I was smooth-
ing my little worm's short white hair and speaking to him thus:

"My little golden tot, you're mine, mine, aren't you? Well,
speak! At least nod your little head!" And I nodded it for him
myself. "There, you see! but how could it be otherwise! After
all, you look absolutely like me and not like Mommy. You don't
have her enormous, saucer-sized eyes, but such tiny ones, intimate, like mine. You have light, sparse locks like I used to have,
and a tiny, round nose like a cherry, just like me —"

There came a dreadful hiss . . . frightened, I looked around to see if there wasn't a snake in the room . . . Helga continued writing peacefully, not raising her eyes . . . And I, although something told me I should leave immediately, carried on, unfortunately, out of a certain reckless spite . . .

"Helmut, precious, why are you looking at Mommy like that? As if you were afraid of her . . . Don't be afraid, she won't do anything to you, and if she wanted to smack you, Daddy wouldn't allow it — after all, you're just completely, completely like me —"

I heard a frightening but muffled noise, like at the circus when a panther roars involuntarily on seeing a burning baton. And suddenly the child's little head disappeared underneath a pillow. It fluttered — — Not knowing what this meant, I looked around and saw Helga — the face of Medusa — holding the infant by the ankle, upside down. And then the little body went flying right over its ghastly mother — I felt a horrible blow and lost consciousness.

On regaining it, I saw my wife sitting on the ground like a Turk and smoking a cigar. Between me and her lay a small naked body motionless, skull shattered. I felt something sticky in my hair and on my face and reached up to it — blood and brains! It took me awhile to understand what had happened, as I was still unable to think straight because of the blow to my skull. And then she spoke, in a calm, terrible, altogether different voice than ever before:

"Since childhood, mysterious powers have intoxicated my soul, bound my will. That's the only way it could have happened that I bound myself to you who are more repulsive to me than anyone. I have shaken them off triumphantly and stand here completely new and strong and terrible; woe to all who stand in my way! You have stained me forever — not by intercourse, but by forcing me to carry your loathsomeness within me for nine months, that it became me and I, it — I could have gone mad! . . . It had to perish! Remember: the nanny let a large gold paperweight fall on its head; if you say any differently, I shall proclaim — there is no witness — that you murdered it! — As of today there will be no exchange of words between us; the most necessary contact shall take place in writing, though not in your handwriting, which makes me want to retch!" And she dashed off.

I shall be as brief as possible. I obeyed her order. The nanny's sentence, at the personal intervention of the emperor, was raised from 4 years to 8. Helga assumed the administration of my property and, I must say, she was good at it. Everyone was terrified of her. Twice I presumed to address her and each time, first drawing on a glove, she answered me with a slap in the face that sent me reeling. The worst thing was that, as time went on, I grew ever more fond of her. For even her external appearance had changed unbelievably; she filled out, grew rosy — she became the most enchanting woman on earth. As long as she was obliging in everything, I paid no attention to her; only now, when she had become unattainable to me, did I pine for her. In my longing for her, a wretched idea occurred to me: "Once she was brought to heel as a result of her father's beating her; perhaps a similar procedure now will render her submissive; although I wouldn't

wish her to fall a second time into her former state of apathy —
but if it turned out even halfway reasonably, that would be the
best thing." And for the first time since the wedding I visited my
charming father-in-law. He consented immediately. I now regret
that I did not portray to him in sufficiently vivid colors the change
his daughter had undergone . . . I was but a meek witness to the
frightful scene which took place the following day. On seeing
his daughter, instead of greeting her the old man struck her across
the shoulders with his scourge — and in the next instant a dagger
drove right through his neck. — After a long struggle with death
he recovered and swore his revenge. One night shortly afterward,
Helga crawled out from the forest on all fours, white as chalk.
She had been shot in the chest. But the next day, her father was
found dead in the forest with a hole in his skull. Helga recovered.
A certain poacher met his end at the hand of the hangman.

From that time on she ceased to concern herself with household affairs and concentrated on other things I prefer not to
mention . . . Shortly thereafter she suddenly went traveling, and
returned only after two years. About all the places she went and
what she did, I know almost nothing. It is said she traveled to the
four corners of the world and, as if the earth were too small for
her, attempted, rumor has it, a trip to the bottom of the ocean,
to the center of the earth from the crater of a volcano, even to
Venus itself. The story was told that she was the leader of a band
of brigands and that she murdered like a doctor. I believe it, for
I know that after her return to Germany she took six murders on
her conscience. And then there were all the other things she did
besides! For example, she founded a clandestine association of the

most beautiful women and adolescent boys, where they cultivated sadism, flagellationism, masochism, lesbianism, fantastical forms of masturbation, sodomy, relations with various animated metal monsters, frightful wax figures, and even with actual specters, etc., etc. But she never had sexual intercourse with men in the usual way, being too contemptuous of them; she did not violate her marital fidelity — and this was the only thing that kept me from punishing her for her godless infamies. Finally, when there had been more than enough of her hell-raising, she was forced at the personal intervention of the emperor to leave his domain. "Your wife's inclinations," he told me, "are understandable, and largely praiseworthy — but you know, dear Helmut — that godless bunch of socialists without a fatherland could be impertinent and make an affaire out of this — we have scandals enough as it is . . . ; you know — have Madame sail to Cameroon for a time! I shall give her my personal letter of recommendation to the governor, so he will supply her there with the black matériel for torture and other diversions, as many as is her wish!" . . . — But the black men did not stimulate her — she considered them half-monkeys, and this degenerate woman never harmed animals; on the contrary, it happened several times that on seeing someone tormenting an animal, she shot the person without ceremony.

When she returned from Africa just half a year later, she brought a fine kettle of fish back with her: a lion, a tiger, a black panther, and a jaguar, altogether magnificent, enormous specimens. She appropriated the greater part of the huge gardens — at least one square kilometer in area, to make a zoo for them. She fed them, so that they would have the pleasure of hunting, live sheep, goats, horses, and bulls; and she even bought them hippopotamuses and rhinoceroses. Sometimes it made for a pretty sight. She would spend whole days in their voluptuous company, always without weapons, usually completely naked. But no one can imagine how they all loved her. When they saw her coming from afar they flew to the bars and roared until all the windows in the chateau rattled. And when she went in to them — what enormous, grotesque leaping there was around her, over her! Looking upon it from outside, though I was trembling, I sometimes burst out laughing. They embraced her, lay down on their backs in front of her like dogs, nuzzled her and licked her — and then roaring in laughter from sheer joy, they at once tussled with each other and in general acted so zanily it was as if they possessed reason. And in zaniness she was not to be outdone by them. She walked on all fours, and tried, the poor woman, to imitate their roars and leaps, scuffled with them, rode on their backs, climbed up in the trees in front of them and leaped down as they caught her in their paws — I'm surprised that all of her ribs weren't broken. She kissed their snouts, she licked their — I won't even say what, she masochistically let them lick her whole body with their prickly tongues until she was completely bloody. And then she — — —. She was eager to have offspring; that according to her caprice, nature would humbly make an exception to its laws. And how she spoke to them! As tenderly as a mother to her infant child. She delivered hour-long lectures to them, on philosophy, God, the concept of the Self . . . And they didn't even budge the whole time, their hellish eyes fixed upon her — no professor of philosophy could have wished for a more appreciative lecture hall.

— But most of all she sang them melancholy songs and — cried, ashamed of doing so — and covered and dried her face with the lion's mane and the tiger's whiskers.

For — she had been transformed! Her wildness had disappeared, and except for her mischief-making with the beasts she no longer kicked up trouble so extravagantly. Constantly lost in convulsions of thought, she merely scribbled and played the piano, badly. For whole days she would run frantically back and forth through the rooms and, as if someone were strangling her, she would howl for whole nights. And she was becoming sadder, more depressed, and worse. She became pale again, and grew thin . . . "May she turn back into a dead puppet!" I exulted to myself. "Then she shall be mine once again! . . . God grant that she become silly again!" — for a secret desire for her flesh was eating at me more and more — and then again, why shouldn't it have? Was it not mine by rights? Was she not mine? What do we have laws for? What do we have church sanctities and sacraments for? I was filled with rage that I wasn't permitted to touch my undisputed property; would it not enrage anyone that he could not enter an apartment he had rented and paid for honestly? What a beggar she was! But — alas! She actually has everything of mine, and I nothing of my own! What good are my boundless riches to me, when but one deadly look from her — and everything is hers? . . .

Once again she stopped speaking, barely ate. She would play with a revolver for hours. "Oh, what shall I do with this life?" I once heard her groan on such an occasion. "Such horrid darkness — darkness everywhere . . . ; is there light anywhere? . . . Ach, there is not! darkness is light, and light darkness. And all is but an abyss of madness . . . O — my Soul. — People say, 'God help me!' But how can *you* help me, who am utterly lacerated? . . . But — — have I not Will? . . . Yet it is even more constricted, more lacerated than any of my animal instincts . . . There is nothing, nothing in it — a rag! . . . Oh why? why? . . . Ach, I know! Because I am a woman, *just a woman!* . . . "

That was how she ranted then — and she continued to wither away . . . "Now is the time!" I finally said to myself, and in a rush of heroism I wrapped my hands around the nape of her neck. In short order I lost my last two front teeth. But she withered away even more . . .

And here she was — 23 years old, it was a brilliant, hot August — and again she underwent a most striking transformation.

Now she was suddenly laughing, leaping about, and even dancing, murmuring joyful songs to herself; she often looked in the mirror, smiled at herself — and was immediately overcome by tears — but they were in no way tragic. She ordered a quantity of exquisite clothes, the finest linens from Berlin: she hadn't looked after herself at all before, often going around dressed like a ragged woman — believing she did not need to enhance her beauty with beautiful clothing. And she became truly kind toward everyone, even friendly; and the most amazing thing was, she even addressed me a few times, and flattered me, of course hardly without irony. Encouraged, I said once: "Helga, is it true that love for me is finally awakening in you?" "Oh, you stupid clod!" she laughed — became merry as an idiot and hopped away.

It seems to me that she was right: perhaps it would never

have occurred to me what the simple reason for all this was, if I had not learned the truth, purely by chance. —

We were living at my castle, Rattentempel, in the Harz Mountains. In an enormous black building, one of the oldest, most impressive medieval monuments in Germany.

On the twelfth of August I was dawdling in the massive castle tower, busying myself with the pigeons. At 2 in the afternoon I saw Helga leave for her usual walk, from which she returned only at night. She was wearing a seductive, light azure dress. I played with the birds for about another half-hour, then by chance I spotted a blue dot in the distance. "It must be her," I said to myself, and I thought it was strange that I could still even see her.

And suddenly, remembering that there was a rather strong telescope in the tower, I had a longing to see her, though far away, just as if she were right in front of me. A moment later I was clearly making out her tigerish, already-flushed profile. She quickly dashed forward, as if she were chasing a hare. I even caught sight of her blissful smile. After a while she began to climb a knoll . . .

I was on the point of tearing my face from the glass — — when I saw on the knoll the figure of a man coming up from the other side. A dark and somehow ghastly thought, I don't know why, went through me: "Fate: why did I not turn my eye from the telescope a second earlier?"

Helga reached the top and suddenly disappeared, as if she had fallen in a hole. A minute later the man also emerged. Helga reappeared, spread her arms — — and fell into his embrace.

This event affected me more powerfully than almost anyone

would have guessed. I have given but little description of all the sufferings my marriage had caused me thus far; in spite of this, probably every reader will say, logically, after all that had already happened, that this event should hardly have fazed me. But feelings are irrationelle, mad; and a wife's unfaithfulness, that most ignominious of things, is always terrible for a husband. My one consolation in all my troubles with her was that until now Helga had not violated her fidelity in another man's embrace; and this one bright point was now extinguished. The whole world leered at me like the night. All the horrible aspects of my bond with this devil rose before me like specters, all the bleak memories descended upon me like swarms of hornets . . . The whole night through, my terrible pain and my still more terrible anger did not let me sleep a wink. I was inflamed with such longing to strangle, slash, and grind into dust that female monster. I swore to wreak the most awful revenge on her . . .

The following day, first thing in the morning, I made my way to that knoll. In the center of the small hilltop was a tiny hollow, overgrown with trampled grass. Inside, it was full of scraps of paper, lace, remnants of food, cigar stubs, bottles full and empty, and so on. Nearby lay two piles of rocks, mostly thin ones, so I was strong enough to lift them. In the smaller heap I found two small, soft, dazzling white, insolent pillows, scourges, whips, and even more unusual sadistic instruments. When I had rolled away a few of the rocks from the larger pile, I saw between them a cavity sufficiently large to hold my small person. Having hollowed it out still more with my hunting knife, I settled down inside it and covered myself back up, after an extended effort, with the displaced rocks. I saw with pleasure that I was well-hidden. One would hardly have known that someone was lying there; and if someone had seen a piece of my clothing, he certainly wouldn't have paid it any attention: the color of the stones was indistinguishable from my clothes. Through my crevice, however, I had an excellent view of the hollow. Filled with an odd, ferocious satisfaction, I returned home.

I was determined to shoot them both from my hiding place; although I sensed I would not find the courage to do so, my passion was oblivious to this.

•

The next morning I left the castle on the pretext of a hunting trip; and an hour before the lovers usually came to the hill, I hid myself there in the rocks again, with a rifle, a revolver, and my knife. But today I had already made up my mind to spare them their lives, at least for the time being, and that I would only watch.

How slowly the time passed for me in my stone straitjacket! My fear was overwhelming, my limbs trembled, my teeth chattered. I was cold, though the sun was scorching hot. I was beginning to feel like throwing off this inhumane bedcover and dashing away . . . ; when Helga's satanic face suddenly sprang up on the edge of the hollow.

She was dressed like Cleopatra, or Semiramis, or some other such harridan . . . It was a miracle she got here at all, through a relatively populated countryside, in such a get-up. She stopped.

She took a drink from a bottle. She took the pillows out from the large pile of stones, tossed them into the hollow, lay down on them, supine, and waving her legs overhead, began to sing, in a Valkyrian voice rolling down from the clouds, a lascivious song beckoning her lover. Then she bounded up, and roaring with both laughter and tears, cried incomprehensible incantations into the winds. She sank back down into the cushions, writhed lecherously, kissed her naked thighs, lashed her calves heartily with a small cane, a black switch she carried with her always, like a dragoon. Again she looked around — :

"He's at the bottom of the hill! . . . Although his wish is that I greet him always completely naked — today I will leave these marvelous clothes on, at least at the beginning, let him thrash me for it, as he likes — — "

And a moment later he appeared. She flung herself on him, rather like a leopard on a hyena . . .

What kind of man was he? A boy, rather younger than she. Truly ugly. I would have found nine out of ten soldiers better-looking than he. But nicely filled out; not thin like her; and when I saw his bare forearm, I shuddered and said to myself: I wouldn't want to fall into his hands . . . But his face? Long, shamefully unkempt hair. He looked like a composer or a poet or some other such good-for-nothing; but even more like a bandit or an international outlaw. And yet at the same time like a child . . . A very strange, abnormal, revolting face! . . . She preferred someone like him over me, a beau in the judgment of all my friends! . . . And he was dressed like a lout besides . . . a battered, muddied coat, torn trousers, a filthy collar, his tie shifted as far as the scruff of his neck, so much sod on his shoes you could have planted potatoes there . . . That, *that* was the kind of man the wife of Germany's foremost aristocrat has chosen, a lady whom even the emperor's princes were shy in courting? But I must say that his impudent, self-confident face so impressed me, that when his commanding eyes looked upon the pile where I was hidden, I huddled involuntarily into a ball . . . Well — an honest person is always afraid of bandits.

I would never have believed that a woman, even one such as Helga, could show her love with such fury! . . . I can't, I don't want to describe it . . . The lout amused himself for a while by playing with her body like with a scrap of rag and grinning. Then he suddenly flung her onto the pillows. And she, before whom even the highest grandees trembled, lay still like a well-trained doggie thrown into the corner — with her little legs up in the air. Only her arms were folded. The rascal flung himself on the ground two meters from her. And then a strange, a most strange conversation took place between them; unfortunately, I was so confused that I can reproduce it only partially. —

They were silent for several minutes; the lout lit up a gypsum pipe from which streamed little black specks. "Speak!" he roared in a voice as suffocating as if it had come from the middle of an empty cathedral; and at the same time he struck her exposed calf with her cane, instantly causing red drops to fall onto the pillow.

"My Only One — You!" howled my trollop without even moving; "I was just thinking: how is it that I always feel as if I were sitting on hot iron when I can't see you, hear you, feel you?

Soon I won't be able to stand it for even a minute without the presence of your body . . . I used to say to myself, if that madness they call love ever possessed me, it would be enough to have His phantasm forever in my soul, then I would be completely with him and be *him* and he with me and be *me*! Only common folk with no imagination and no spirit need the touch of a coarse body to feel and to see, to hear with their own coarse ears that coarse, material voice . . . — because, darling, your voice is so vulgar next to the archangels' music of the spheres, which is your every breath in my dreams; and — how truly ugly you are next to the terrible, seraphic, metamystical dragons that visit me and kiss me so sweetly every night — this is You! — Yet — in spite of all this, I must have you always in my eyes and ears . . . I — —. Love is vulgarity: the greatest of all! Anyone who falls in love ceases to be human, Will dissolves in its mire. No madhouse is mad enough for one in love. Anyone who falls in love should be hung immediately. There is no corner on earth that would admit such an outcast. Death is the only salvation. Better to drop dead than to become the disgrace that is lov–"

— "woman!" he yawned.

"Of course, you don't love me, eh, do you? You don't have to have me always at your side, eh? It's enough for you to dream about me and masturbate, eh? All I'm good for is flogging, eh? Well say it, say it, so I can finally shoot myself!"

"Always and forever stupid!" hissed that jack of spades. "This love of yours is the same for all female goods without exception, and for 98 percent of men, or rather for degenerate women. You can tell a real Man by the fact that this is not his way. My attraction to you has a bestial force — you're a damned slippery, seductive beast, I'd never have thought that anything on this lousy earth could attract me so . . . except the earth itself. O repulsive mire! . . . But I couldn't help saying to myself: if this despicable pressure on me grows by even a hair — we'll never see each other again! Love is a dog; if it obeys, it's good, if not, if it tries to go for my throat — I'll strangle it! Girl, I go in for somewhat higher things than female haunches. All you are for me is the best roast there is, but my life isn't all food."

"I know that, I know, my Majesty, my Holy One!" she humbly fawned upon that boorish delinquent. "And it's absolutely enough for me. It's just that, if you feel something tender and true toward me . . . I don't want you to be like a woman, like a slave, my Sovereign! A Man only plays with a woman, ravishes her and crushes her . . . But he has to do it thoroughly: only then does he love her in a manly way, with dignity — only then does *she* love him like a woman — —"

And having given him a strong birch rod, she rolled over onto her stomach. With a single crack he tore off her expensive garment with the gold and diamond stars woven into it so that only shreds remained. And he gave her about forty of them, and what blows! It would have left me dead! She hissed a little and yowled, but nothing could be heard except for the swishing of the rod; she shook her behind, which for the first time I saw naked that day — but not even once did she try to protect it with her hands . . .

Then, covering her crimson, wet, twisted face with a hand-kerchief, she crept up to the lout on her knees and lay her head on his stomach. Like a dog . . .

"If I spoke the language of God, I could not express my thanks to you! You have given me everything, everything, and I am completely, only yours and your property! Night was I, you have made it into day. Empty was I, and you have filled me to overflowing with gold and diamonds and scents. Out of pure pain and loathing, I was formed by the devil's hand. A roaring Niagara of ever-lethal delight and Blessing, rushing — not down — upward into all the Heights, this you have made of me. Every speck of dust I see is for me a ray from the Eye of God! Every thought an uncanny, magical blossom. From the lowest of beggar-women you have made an empress of empresses — no less! from a slimy little worm — a Goddess. — What is that idiot Homer's bland, lifeless Hera or Aphrodite next to me?"

"Well, don't I always tell you that you're my little stupid piggy!" he growled and rolled her around, back and forth, inquisitively, like a lion turning over a captive human with its paw, not knowing if he's still alive or dead. And my charming little missus let herself be rolled about like a rolling pin for making noodles, and she continued in a soft whisper, wrapping her wounds with what was left of her garment.

"Yes I am! A piggy, a bitch, an earthworm — — a female! A compost heap from which rotten children grow. Disgusting! We're zeroes. Only when a man is put before us does a zero start to have worth. Creeping plants: without you we have no purpose whatsoever. We are 1/10; man, 9/10. It would make sense if every man trampled down every woman without further ado. Even the lowest, puniest man is greater than the greatest woman — don't grin, you're still just a boy! But you are a Man, the greatest man, the only true man. You alone have character, self-awareness, Will that truly commands; you always do only what you want; you are never passive. You alone stand firm while the rest of humanity reels about drunkenly. You are my Napoleon — you know how much you resemble Guérin's portrait of him? — but you have something more spiritual in your face, though nothing like Hamlet . . . But I, I am the puniest, sorriest shred of a woman on earth! You have no idea!" She burst into tears. "I am regarded everywhere as a miracle of womanly strength, a flame of bravery — and what am I? A slattern, a slut, just a rag tossed by black, mysterious windstorms . . . I'm not even human, just a grotesque machine; no, how I have flattered myself, the sovereign Game — mere child's play! O my rock of granite, at least you used to consider me strong. But how can one be strong who, like me, a child, went out of her senses for a period of many years — and when I awoke, it was only that I might go mad —"

"Tell me your life story, at last! As concisely as possible!"

"I will. Concisely. You are the first and the last who will hear it! —

— "My childhood was very unusual, my upbringing, one of a kind. My father — he wasn't as much of an eccentric then as he became later, although from birth an enormous misanthrope — he had just one dream: to sire an offspring who would be as energetic, independent, heroic, fiery, wild, immoral as possible. He was not disappointed in me; I was good raw material for his naturally somewhat unskilled hands. He raised me with remarkable boldness, as perhaps no child has ever been raised; not so that I might become a sheep, a good little cluck, but a terrible eagle, a lioness. You are not one of those morons who'd say at this point: that's why she turned out that way, brought up like that; what I am, I would be under any circumstances; but perhaps I grew a good deal taller under a favorable sun than would have happened under the clouds of an ordinary, swinish upbringing.

"He loved me; only me on this earth; he disdained all people — excepting, poor man, himself; and only in me did he see himself. His love, his tender, childlike love toward me was just as intense as his harsh brutishness toward everyone else . . . If he punished me, it was only because in his judgment I was too tame, lacking in courage, too considerate. I loved him, I'm not ashamed of it . . . But today, in spite of the fact that I killed him, I still harbor a deathly hate for him — oh! oh! . . . I have scorned all people like insects, only in him did I see a human being — myself.

"But also in my mother. A sleepwalker, spectral, always brooding, but not a weak creature; and beautiful as a fallen angel; — yet — if she were alive, I'd kill her today, just like I killed him . . . The way he raised me certainly wasn't much to her liking; she cried over my mischievousness, but said: it is just an expression of the All-Encompassing Nature of God, and anyone who opposed it would be opposing God . . . If she punished me sometimes, it was because I wasn't reading assiduously enough the various faddish, mystical books that she, poor woman, treasured above all else. Naturally, I held it against her just as little as I did against my father if he punished me for making a deep curtsy before his boss, the colonel.

"Then the day came; I had just turned ten. A few days before, having made a bet with my girlfriends, I walked across the square at noon completely naked. My father found out that day. He chortled with glee, kissed me, and had me smoke from his pipe.

"There was a great scandal. My father got an awful reprimand at headquarters, and — inasmuch as he wouldn't hold his tongue — pensioned off. But I found this out only eight years later.

"Misera mens humana! Having returned from the colonel, like a bolt from the blue he tied me to the bench and lashed me cruelly. In and of itself that would have been nothing — but the awful thing was, that in his vociferation, he now spoke to me in the same way as all those other respectable people whom he had always described to me as insects, here only to be stepped on and squashed . . . ; with this my ideal, in one fell swoop, had become the scabbiest reptile . . . Do you understand?

"And still, what I had done was no worse than my many previous escapades, which he had welcomed with joy, although they caused him enormous difficulties. And now, all at once — — he had fallen! He had betrayed *himself.* A weak man . . . At most, he was angry; perhaps there was even some sadism in it; I would have more than forgiven him this; but under no circumstances should rage determine the actions of a Man. No, a Man should never, ever be enraged; you, boy, I have never seen enraged. If Napoleon had fallen into a rage for even one minute, a real one, he would never have even gotten as far as Toulon. In my father I saw more than Napoleon; and now, by the force of contrast, I see the biggest jerk in the world . . .

"When he untied me, I flew in desperation to my mother, who had witnessed the thrashing and said nothing. I instinctively sought in her a refuge where I would again find faith in something, anything at all . . . 'Speak, Mommy, say something to him! He's gone mad, he's simply gone mad!'

"To this day I would still love to know how she would have behaved if my infuriated father had not screamed:

"'You show her good and proper that her parents stick together, you show her how to deal with such a spoiled, perverse reject!'

"And then she — lashed me hardly less severely than he, and what was worse, she accompanied it with the words: 'You harlot, you shameless girl' — etc . . . She forgot — that female creature, about her 'expressions of God'! . . . That's why she died a year later — —

"It is impossible to describe how I felt. — An hour afterward I was rolling on the floor, howling with desperation and breaking everything around me. But those two blackguards evidently had some sort of mystical respect for that and slunk off somewhere . . . All became for me the darkest night — do you know what it is to be absolutely disillusioned? . . . Of course, a ten-year-old girl couldn't stick up for herself on her own — but you told me, darling, to be as concise as possible!

"In my boundless night something intensely white suddenly came drifting toward me. It had no shape, and yet it did. A wisp of fog? An animal? A person? A rose? A star? . . . I don't know. It was as sweet as it was frightening . . . And it gave me a kiss on my forehead. 'Sleep, sleep, my child! Sink into a long, deep slumber! No one needs sleep more than you, so that you might be strengthened for your pilgrimage through eternity, Your pilgrimage to me! Sleep, my child, sleep!' — And after it kissed me, I felt an enormous relief — and I heard something burst in my brain, so nicely and smoothly, so delicately, it burst so painlessly, like when you break a thin film of ice under water. And then — I no longer know.

"Our respected scientists would explain the whole thing by saying that some blood vessel had burst in my skull as a result of my rage, and that the hemorrhaging in my brain made me crazy. But I know that it was the kiss of that White — Something that did it. The brain, the nerves, the body are nothing other than the crude, material visibility of that which goes on in the soul. If a small vein had burst, it was the cause of nothing; it was the result of something else; my soul had collapsed — and that must be visible even with miserable eyes and microscopes. The universe is the mere, incorporeal shadow of the Soul. —

"I lived in a kind of indescribable half-dream for eight years; a little like when you're falling asleep or ever-so-slowly waking up. I was somnambulating. I have no recollection of my mother's death or even of my father's beating me day after day to try and shake me out of it. Or even of — but you ordered that my story be concise.

"When did I begin to awaken? . . . The first time — it was only a foretaste: that time when Mr. Revolting pressed me to himself while dancing and said — I don't even remember — the most nauseating thing to me . . . Something unfamiliar suddenly spurted up inside me. An inkling of the future, it was . . . But just as when a single lightning flash tears through a black night, it disappeared, and it was night once again.

"I began to feel that way constantly — oh! with my pregnancy

. . . It began to grow in my wretched, sleeping soul — deep down, somewhere down deep . . . the strangest kind of revulsion . . . I wasn't aware of my embryo, only of this revulsion. And it grew and grew. And beneath its hellish, warm breath my numbed soul began to thaw. Ever so slowly. A revulsion with myself and at something foreign to me. Was it I, was it something else? But this was the most revolting thing: I didn't know it . . . A vile, terrifying dragon from down below . . . — it would have devoured anyone else, but there was nothing left of me to devour . . . So it gave birth — — to me! . . . I am the child of revulsion — and nothing more! But not even you can understand this! Only the abysses of Dreams sometimes whisper something similar — exploding and then, immediately extinguished, forgotten . . .

"Finally, the revulsion issued from me. Nonetheless, it stayed within me — the head of a tapeworm. My soul felt a great relief, greater than my body, but only because now my revulsion became suddenly active: as I lay absolutely passive beneath its immense belly, it no longer — *controlled* me; although it tossed me about more than previously, my awakened will wrestled with it — an equal opponent; that is true right up to today. And this revulsion has transformed itself into a raging hatred. *A hatred of revulsion* and a revulsion of hatred — for nothing is more revolting than hatred: this is the mystery of my entire existence. This has dictated all my subsequent behavior: a murderous, revulsion-filled enmity — toward everything that is outside myself —"

"You stupid goose, what can there be that's outside of you?"

"You're right, as always . . . There is nothing outside the self — and everything that whimpers slavishly within me: 'something exists outside of You' is only an infernal trick of this very Self. Oh, how I look forward to thoroughly discussing this important question with you — there in the Cordilleras — my little phantom, paradoxically wiser than I! Aw, don't sulk, your little bitchy-poo will be concise — she *is* a treasure, isn't she? I'll get to the point!

"I said: what is 'outside myself'; but no matter what you do, you always feel that there is something in You that somehow You are not. We are only worms; we don't have it in us to consider, like Berkeley, every silly visual, aural sensation to be an indifferent dream, Our Little Game, the plasma of Our Will — we submit to them! Don't sulk — you're a guy — a woman is always more mature, I know more than you," and she began half-jokingly, half-seriously to beat his skull with her fists. During all this he didn't even so much as take his pipe out of his gob and just kept grinning; — finally he threw her at least five meters to the side, so that she flew through the air like a ball. She crawled back to him on her knees and picked up her story:

"It's difficult to be concise when we're talking about the essence of our life. Before —: I killed that little revulsion in self-defense: otherwise it would have killed me. I killed my father — that lunatic, he had to go! I would have shown him mercy if he had appeared before me not with his belts but with memories of his ruined military career . . . That left Mr. Revolting; the only thing that has saved him thus far is the fact that I loathe the idea of squishing that hideous caterpillar. And those others whom I have killed or tortured were also only the victims of my bestial Hatred; never of sadism: that presupposes love. My polypous tentacles have never embraced either a man or the most beautiful woman with such warmth that I could take delight in their squirming. It's all been sunless revulsion . . . That's why I went mad, in every way, so I could escape my revulsion, my revolting self. Do you know whom you've fallen in love with? The most foul-smelling swamp. I am Vileness incarnate."

"You're an attempt at an ingenious woman," he mumbled, deep in thought. "Perhaps the first such one . . . This is what'll probably happen with women in a hundred thousand years —"

"Yes, darling, you taught me that . . . One is obliged to wade through hatred and revulsion to reach the heights of Blessedness, Smiling, Laughter, All-Embracing, Self-Embracing. Eagles and condors have arisen from slimy lizards . . . But when will this happen with me? Darling, when I began to rage, I had no doubts that I was something supreme, that I had the highest, divine Will, which does with everything quodlibet; and all those people on their knees before me confirmed it. As long as I believed this, I was still something magnificent . . . And with the decline of this faith, which started in Cameroon, all my virtue disappeared. I finally understood that my 'will' was marvelous only when it was the blind servant of my blind instincts; but there is no more amusing contradiction than: a will that serves —: Will and the Absolute Mistress, or God, are one and the same. I understood that, since my passions tossed me about more than anyone else — that magnificent will of mine was in reality more enslaved, i.e., more worthless than that of any Flossie from the cowshed. I saw myself as the most contemptible, because the weakest, monster on earth. And at that time I also said to myself what I told you just a short while ago: 'You must wade through the deepest swamp to reach the Highest Radiance — once in a million years; this life of yours is the basest thing of all — — and must end terribly!'"

"You always draw your bow so tightly in everything, girl, like a lunatic. But *that* is why you're truly in danger of crashing! And I'm almost afraid that the snapped bowstring, the exploded rifle, will take me apart as well —"

"But what do you mean! Little me — You!" And she curled herself up into him as if she were an unhappy child who wanted to hide herself from the cruel, foul gales of this world back in her mother's womb . . . "But what does such a glimpse into eternity mean for a little beast like me, completely swept away in the space of a second! What for You is everything, for me has been, and perhaps still is, nothing at all! —

"Revolted with myself, I was deprived of all the black strength of my hatred, my only strength! And the old, stagnantly passive revulsion came back — and it almost seemed as if I would again fall into a stupid half-dream . . . Then You came along! And suddenly everything changed! You gave me nothing — only insults and beatings! you took nothing from me, although I — beggar that I am, having nothing better, placed a hundred million on your palm! But — I love You!" and she broke down into sobs, the harlot. "Now I believe in God, or whatever it is, only because out of millions of people he allowed me to know — You, the Man of all men! — By your breath my night has suddenly, as if on the equator, become day; the nocturnal toad has become a nightin-gale; the ill-fated alligator of the marshy pool a shining eagle. My hatred has almost dissolved into love for everything, excepting —

him . . . I embrace all, understand all, see all — I, who once was blind; O miraculous doctor, giving sight to those blind from birth! All is Mine! I am capable of everything on Earth under your command. I have ideas and feelings like no one has ever had before. I feel the strength to create works greater than any of those with which the civilization of wretched humanity glitters. Thus far I have lived in the external world, on the surface, I called it 'action,' tried to convince myself that 'deeds' were the greatest: no, it is creative works! or actually, not creative works: ideas, such as thunder in the soul! Or no, not ideas: Will, from within its own cathedral, unmoved by anything exterior to it, kneeling before itself, worshipping only itself, not needing ideas — which are only the concerns of a pitiful beast — man —: it is the eternal Divine Self-Embrace in a metamystical Radiance. But what is *your* opinion of that? Which is greater, action or thought? You haven't told me yet what your goal actually is. Do you want to become a Napoleon? Or a bandit chief? Or a thinker? artist? explorer?"

"All superficial concepts, created by narrow, vain, ambitious men. I don't want to become: I *am!* and not nothing, but everything. There is no human greatness that I would not see as beneath myself and my game. My will does and shall do all with everything. If they try to pigeonhole me as a brigand or a philosopher, if they say I have been nothing, or a god, or a swine — they are but human wretches! I am who I am, I do what I want, I want infinitely all!"

"You are God!" she cried and kissed the ragamuffin's boots, shot through with holes, and the muddy fringes of his trousers. "Thus speaks the 'Consummate Victor!' But we who are not yet ready must concentrate on ending our squalor. And I want to concentrate myself completely on spirituality, on what is most ethereal, and to throw over everything earthly, coarse, action-oriented, scheming. To live only in God, to be only God, but only ever in Your shadow! Oh, that most radiant future that rises before me like a sun! In the Cordilleras, right beneath the eternal glaciers, we will carve out a palace for ourselves, the Residence of residences — of the two greatest people, two gods! Circled by friendly, sweet condors in flight, and fed by our eagle and snake, like Zarathustra! Chasms below us, the chasm of the heavens above us, chasms within us — and all of them bridged by our supra-solar Will and set thundering in a Hymn of Eternal Victory! . . . I will be pure love, love, Love — for You, for everything, for Myself, — and for my hatred! But, my Glorious One, Divine One — if I myself do not reach this heaven — our children shall! Oh! What children we two shall have, rulers of the earth and thought! For — even I'm not just anyone! I used to curse myself like a sailor, but you know a woman's logic; I consider myself in spite of everything the greatest female monstrosity on earth and I'll tell you: I'm no worse than you: even if you're stronger than I, I'm richer, go ahead and smack me a couple of times for that! I will bear *You* children till I drop, though the whole thing has seemed to me so awfully disgusting till now — because instead of Men I have known only stupid milksops. But the first child that comes along — you must grant me this, otherwise I will never be happy — I will put to death; quite painlessly, with a narcotic. It probably has something to do with that earlier, nameless revulsion, it almost certainly does. But I know that it will take along with it all of the stench from me — that only afterward will I be completely purified, that only then will I bear children — that are truly Yours! . . . Do you consent?"

"Of course, my silly little piggy."

And I, I just chewed my lips. "So you want to be unfaithful to me? to have bastard children?" I just couldn't believe it! Until now she had been a model spouse. Such lyrical outbursts as she was boring that vagabond with meant nothing more than burping and belching. And if he flogged her, good for him! let him cultivate that scoundrel's rump for me, if I can't! let him teach her! And that he saw her, by now completely naked — dear me! after all, the sun, which had heated the rocks over me until I was half roasted, was also gazing upon her; and that he was groping her here and there, dear me! every little blade of grass she lay on was touching her; and those four noisy beasts were doing the same thing in my gardens. It was all a trifle! She was just prattling away to him, I knew; when it came right down to it, she would remain faithful to me!

And then the ragamuffin put aside his old pipe, wound his arm around my lawful wife, and smacking her everywhere, spoke more tenderly than before:

"You're my dear little silly piggy, but a megathere too. The most vulgar and the most celestial simmer within you, a devilish cauldron, you little Daemoness of mine! Both in the greatest doses. Water and fire; a cauldron filled to bursting with foul water, a solar fire that would heat a cauldron fifty times bigger. It will surely burst, although now *I* am operating the machine.

"And — your baseness is stronger than your greatness. You are the slave of your instincts, however sublime they may be, but even the most sublime instinct is still base. If your will were to triumph over them — you'd be saved — for this life! Otherwise you shall die, very soon and very horribly. A cadaverous smell emanates from you . . . It irritates me, but O cadaverous smell, may you become the scent of a rose! . . .

"Even your baseness is sublime! You are Sublime! Fate has made of you its most frightful plaything; there has never been one like it! Therefore I love you . . . But fate evidently intended to break its plaything after it had had enough of it — and in order to have still more fun with it . . . You live only for your intéressantness.

"You are damned, more than any being that is human; and for this very reason you are called above all others. Only the damned are called.

"But there is still hope — scant . . . And I don't want you to abandon me, not *here* . . . better that the sun should be extinguished — ugh! I might seem sentimental . . . Except for you everything is human sludge — ugh! . . .

"And yet if you triumph — this will be *my* most enchanting triumph! If I do not achieve this — perhaps I shall fall with you . . . For I love *you* — — listen!

"You require the greatest Self-Mastery; otherwise your powerful night will master You in the end — and you shall die. Only what travels toward the Light, in its own way, remains alive; all else dies! at the appointed time.

"Your appointed time: the next five days! . . . — we leave for the Cordilleras on the nineteenth —"

"The nineteenth?" she shrieked like a maenad. "Is that an order? The most beautiful day of my life — so soon? . . ."

"On the fourth afternoon — be here, and we shall go — —"

Screaming with delight, she embraced him with her legs. He continued:

"Your appointed task for the next five days: you will conduct yourself as humanely as possible with Sternenhoch! In nothing will you offend him — and in parting, you will give him a kiss lasting half a minute!"

"For God's sake — what do you want of me? Order me to cut up my entire face right now with this knife, have me disfigure myself for life — and I will do so at once, obediently . . . But that?"

"I know it's difficult, the most difficult of all. But it's necessary to make a frontal attack on the enemy's center! No skirmishing like a tirailleur!"

"But — but — I'll destroy all of my past life with this —"

"It must be destroyed!"

"I'd die at once if I did this."

"Your death shall be more terrible and protracted if you do not!"

"— My Master — — — that is — yes — agh! no, no! — Master! — — y– y– — yes! . . . I will do it!" She exhaled from deep within herself . . . "But — how harsh you are!"

"Merciful. Fate is harsh as a rule, for the baseness of created beings deserves nothing more. Enough! I have spoken!"

"Your will be done!" she whispered. "But permit me one more word: You don't know, you don't know what will come of this, in this you are a fool. If I do this, I'll be tearing myself up from my roots —"

"The universe must be torn from its roots!"

"Very well. Then I'll tear myself up and drop dead."

"You shall triumph or fall. I know You . . . — Your consorting with him is the most revolting thing I have heard of; this is why revulsion controls you from within itself. The basest thing of all is hatred and revulsion; to what I hate and find repulsive, I am the most terrible slave. This hate-filled canaille ought to be — My mistress? . . . If this is not carried out, the nineteenth will be the last time we see each other!"

"May Your Will come to pass!" — —

They fell silent. And I was losing consciousness because of my unnatural position, the pressure of the stones, the forced, complete immobility, the heat, thirst, fury, hatred, fear, and every possible hellish feeling. Oh, why had I dared attempt this! — Should I stand up erect and punish them terrifically? . . . Wait until they left? But it was only five o'clock and they always stayed here until sundown. A terrible situation . . .

The silence was interrupted by this:

"I've had a feeling that someone's been watching us. Hey, girl! From that tower of yours we could be seen rather well by telescope."

"You mean — by Mr. Revolting? What would that matter?"

And just then his terrible eyes pierced directly into mine. I shuddered. But it was impossible, wholly impossible for him to make them out in the dim light through a centimeter-wide crevice.

"Someone could hide fairly well over there between those rocks," he said offhandedly, lighting his pipe again.

"Like Mr. Revolting? You think he would dare do that? Ha ha! You haven't the slightest idea what a scared old lady he is! A rabbit is a lion next to him, that mangy dog —"

She got a slap, a solid one all right. "Is this how you begin to fulfill your promise? For those of us who aren't mangy dogs, broad-mindedness toward such a wretch is a command. Don't you know that the first rule for any more reasonable person is parcere subjectis et debellare superbos? — And remember: even the doggiest of dogs gets rabid."

"But he is worse than any dog — excuse me," she laughed, protecting her face. "From now on I shall call him 'panthère,' 'my dearest panthère'! But I also thought I just saw those rocks over there move, somehow —."

She was getting up. My eyes grew dark, my ears were full of a sound like the roar of a stormy sea.

"Lie down!" he said and pulled her back. And she humbly lay down. He grinned strangely. He knew, he certainly knew, the lout, that I was lying there; it's a riddle to me why he continued not to notice me. But he was certainly afraid of the terrible revenge of a cuckolded husband.

"Lie down and better take a look around: some people are coming toward us, and you're naked."

"When they come closer, shoot them without further ado!" and she gave him the revolver.

"What's the point of making such a racket?" He went up to the edge of the hilltop and made a couple of peculiar, commanding movements with his arms, wordlessly. "They're going down again," he growled after a while, and added:

"Let's leave!"

"Now, Master?" She was frightened.

"I don't feel like staying here any longer today. Let's go into the forest."

"But before that — — at least for a moment . . . please! This entire time I've been seeing — —." And she pointed in some direction . . .

The ragamuffin stood for a moment, apparently undecided. Then his eyes met mine again, a mocking spark twinkled in them. He laughed and lay down.

— —

The last point of light in the sky flickered out; the blackest night flooded my soul. —

I don't understand how I survived the next few moments. Fortunately they didn't last long. If those two scum had waited a second longer to disappear, something terrible would have happened.

Completely naked, draped all over that lout, leaping and dancing and singing triumphantly, she pranced off into the countryside.

The measure of your iniquities, you adulteress, you stain upon the earth, is filled. This "mangy dog" will show you! And you, you stinking rogue, shall not savor her impure, slimy, disgusting body for long! You have only my boundless kindness and magnanimity to thank that, having been infuriated like a terrifying angel of revenge, I did not immediately carry out the most frightening judgment upon you! But it will be all the more terrible for this! You swine! You snivelling scoundrel! You slinking whore — you — — you — — —

II

On the 19th of August, Helga really did disappear —. I don't
know where — — —

August 25

Something terrible happened the day before yesterday. That —
— of hers visited me yesterday at the castle. But I cannot, cannot
entrust this to paper . . . perhaps later . . .

— — — — — — — — — — — — — — — — — — — —

October 16

Oh, what a terrible two months I have had! It is a miracle that I
haven't gone mad; but I have one foot already over the threshold
of madness. An indescribable horror — sympathy — compa–
— but I daren't write it, paper is a perfidious blackguard, such
words already — —

Thank God relief has come; my condition is improving from day to day, I'm beginning to forget — oh Lord, stay by my side!

October 24

The treatment is continuing; I have been feeling well the last two days and almost as happy as a year ago. The struggle is over.

October 27

Something awful happened, unthinkable, impossible. My hair is still standing on end. I caught sight of — Her! It was yesterday at the court ball. Weary from the dancing, the music, the thronging of people, to distract myself I withdrew from the hall at midnight through a series of rooms, stretching further and further away into the distance. There were thirteen of them. Do you know the strange feeling that overcomes you as you draw further and further away from dazzling lights, the hum of a thousand voices, a hall pealing with music? The sounds grow frightfully weak, fewer and fewer people are seen around you in the rooms, which gradually become smaller and smaller, the mysterious desolateness more and more evident, finally the music is almost inaudible, and it seems as if you have fallen into a world of specters, into a sorceror's chambers, teeming with invisible spirits . . .

The tenth room was entirely empty. The door to the eleventh was closed. I turned the handle, it opened — there were two frightened shrieks — and what did I see? On the divan sat Admiral von M., a ladies' hat on his bald pate, and in his lap he was holding His Excellency the Minister of War, who was toying with a ladies' lace handkerchief. They bounced up, white as paper, and their legs were shaking so much that they fell to their knees. "Ah, ah, ah!" the admiral finally yelped, "how fortunate that it is only you, Your Excellency! And I would swear that I had locked the door with the key!" "God has had mercy on us!" the minister blurted out through chattering teeth, and in a flash he locked the door with the key. "Come join our little circle, mon prince!" the admiral invited me, "tres faciunt collegium." Paying them not the slightest attention, I made only a haughty, dismissive gesture and went on. "Our prince is musing and pondering," I heard behind me in a respectful low whisper — the fellows well aware of my importance in the emperor's circles; "he's a great thinker, another Kant . . ." I entered the twelfth room, which was empty. Taking up a position by the window, I peered out into the terrible, starry night, the hours ghostly striking midnight from the tower . . . I pulled myself together suddenly, as if disturbed from sleep, and headed into the thirteenth, final room. Something horrid, a silence like the grave, came over me; but, feeling as if I were drugged, I told myself, from a pedantic caprice, that I must walk to the end of the outermost chamber, which was a dead end, which had always, whenever I visited it previously, filled me with a mystical fear. I opened the door leading into it — — and before me stood Helga. None other than she. I shall not describe her gaze as she looked at me, for I cannot . . . I sank and remained sitting on the threshold; whether for a long or a short time, I do not know; my consciousness had become merely black circles, having horribly deluged both her and the whole room . . . — Finally I felt some pressure on my shoulder — and recognized the minister and the admiral. "For the love of God, what is His Excellency up to here?" said the minister, wringing his hands. I stirred slowly, and not yet quite myself, I walked back. "Ah! I understand!" whispered the admiral obsequiously behind me, slapping his forehead. "Socrates, if taken up by some problem, would stand still as a statue for whole hours, wherever he may have been, whether on a stepladder or in a public place; but our prince is still wiser: he sits down comfortably in the meantime!" — Only after I had reached the ballroom did I recall clearly what I had really seen. Escorted by my two friends, I walked about in the gathering for a long time — nowhere was there a face similar to Hers. I repaired with them to the thirteenth room — nowhere a trace of Her! The minister and the admiral saw no one. She couldn't have escaped through the windows of the last two rooms: they were all closed from within. Did she perhaps disappear through some secret passage in the wall? or wriggle through the keyhole — — but what am I saying — like a madman — — what horrors — I must stop . . . —

October 28

Oh, whatever was it? Helga, alive, real? or merely my hallucination? or — — Her ghost? . . . Well — it's out: I'm afraid that she's dead, that she came to me — that she's going to come again and again to keep haunting me . . . Why would she be dead? Eh, I don't know, I don't know anything, it's just . . . And I also don't know what would be more frightening: if she were alive or if she were a ghost . . . But the most frightening thing is the uncertainty. Oh, oh! All night I heard an awful rustling next door to my bedroom — only I don't know for sure if it was Helga or a mouse . . .

All Souls' Day was terrifying — but today I'm all right again. I had come to the incontrovertible certainty that she had been a mere delusion of mine, a purely clinical hallucination, perfectly explicable by my prolonged agitation and my endlessly envisioning that hellcat in my imagination: her image simply leapt from my overexcited brain onto my retina; why wouldn't it have, if the same thing can happen in normal seeing? — The thing is not to be startled and everything will be all right.

December 1

Everything is all right. It's true I have to drink and carouse constantly in order not to think about a certain — a certain something, but I'm no longer having any hallucinations, I'm not afraid of them, I'll never be afraid of them again.

December 3

Today, at two in the afternoon, I went for a walk in the woods near my chateau at Saustein, where I most like to reside. No trace of snow anywhere; the earth as green as in April; the sun shone as if it were March, warming, almost scorching. It was one of those dreadfully entrancing winter days when nature, dead and yet alive, gives the impression of a naked, galvanized corpse. I was strolling dreamily through the snowy, quietly resplendent glade, warm in my heart. At this point I caught sight of, off to the side in the forest, on a bench by the footpath, a lady's dress, twinkling dazzlingly on a dark background, casting a long, black shadow in the low sun. I love the ladies and thus, having gone around the other way, I set out on that footpath and approached the bench. I was already standing next to it when I saw — — Helga! . . . Just as when I was on the threshold earlier, I now sat right down on a pile of leaves . . . But today I suddenly acquired a stoutness of heart — I jumped up and scrambled headlong out of there, screaming with horror. From behind me I heard, in a terrible voice: "You old hag! scoundrel! bastard!" — and also the rapid stomping of footsteps. It was a miracle I didn't die of fright. — "You thought you were rid of me, but I'm going to keep on hounding you! Ha ha ha, you bastard, ha ha ha!" it roared, like the guffawing of a wood sprite. I kept running until I was out of the forest; then I sank onto the grass. But a moment later, a rustling sound came from out of the forest; perhaps it was a hare, a bird, or a squirrel, but I lit out of there. Finally I looked around. No one was following me. "I'm safe!" I sighed; and the joyous, warming glow of the sun filled me with delight, pride, and a heroic feeling. Then I looked — and saw Helga about 200 paces ahead of me, moving in my direction. She was coming exactly from where I had been fleeing to — it would have been impossible for her to outrun me so quickly by coming the long way around. I started to make my escape off to the side — but at that moment, praise God, two old ladies with kindling-wood on their backs came my way. "I'm among people, I'm safe!" I cried out, filled with happiness, and I embraced the old women and kissed them. Then I looked back — I no longer saw Helga. The old women had to escort me as far as the chateau, and each of them was rewarded 1000 marks for it. —

I felt she would hound me forever. Of course, it was only my empty, wretched hallucination. But, damn it all, what's the use of my knowing that when it causes me the same horror, when it could drive me just as mad as a real ghost? When in the moment I experience it, I have to regard it as her very spirit? A hallucination, it seems to me, is only another, less honest word for what all our wise forefathers called a "ghost"; it's all the same. Oh God, my God — —

December 4

But is it so certain that it was a hallucination yesterday, i.e., a ghost? Couldn't it have been — Helga, alive, in the flesh? At least that one in the forest might well have been. Of course, I can't explain how she could have outrun me so quickly; but did I really recognize the face of the one who approached me in the fields? And any lady could have had on such an outfit . . .

Yet how could she have turned up here, when for the last three and a half months she has been in — — the Cordilleras? . . . And she surely must have broken her neck there, I ask you, such mountains as those! . . . But it can't be entirely ruled out that — — she didn't break it — she could have esca– come back. After all, there's certainly a capital cold there now — — —

Anything is possible. The one yesterday could have been for real, the one in the thirteenth room a hallucination — the one doesn't exclude the other. I really don't know anything for sure. Ghastly uncertainty, enough to drive one mad . . . I could destroy her — — and I know how — I know, I won't tell anyone — but it would be too horrible — no, no! . . .

December 6

But the uncertainty is still more horrible . . . I must — but I
cannot — — no — no — Merciful Lord!

December 8

I caught sight of her again! Today in the town of R., two hours
journey from my chateau. In a crowded street; right at noon. She
was walking with a lady and two gentlemen; one of them had
treated me some time ago for lues, and I also know that other
lady, from a nightclub. She spoke with them sonorously in that
demonic voice of hers so familiar to me. They replied to her
briskly, as if to any other mortal. She didn't even glance at me
. . . although I was forced to sit for a while on some sacks of
coal stacked up on the side.

   She's alive, she's alive! that's for sure! . . . How were those
people able to speak with her, and even laugh with her? She's alive
— she *escaped* from — — the *Cordilleras.* In the brightness of
noontime — on the main promenade — with spiffy dressers —
she had a lorgnon — what kind of normal ghost or hallucination,
for God's sake, needs a lorgnon? . . . But how the deuce could she
have — — come back — from the Cordilleras? . . .

December 9

But is it so certain that she was for real? Her escorts could also
have been my hallucination, just as she was. And if they weren't,
she could also have been their hallucination, just as she was mine.
And well, a thousand devils, that whole noisy little street and
even the clear, low sun could have been only a vile hallucination.

Anyhow, the whole universe is just a hallucination, and most of all, so am I.

From afar the winds of — madness — are again beginning to blow over me. I have a talent for it, a certain reputable doctor once told me. I have had those, those, begging your pardon, hallucinations many times before, but they were otherwise innocent; e.g., I once watched my dog, Napoleon, playing with a bitch in a closed room for half an hour. All at once I gave a start, rubbed my eyes — and Napoleon was lying down and sleeping, and the bitch was nowhere in sight; she couldn't have escaped, the doors were locked from inside. And this is not a little bitch-pup here, but a devil incarnate — a Daemoness. It had already happened once before: Prince Sternenhoch had married Satan . . .

I must find out for certain! I must! Tomorrow I will go to the castle, where that tower is with the telescope. — Hoo — oo — — oooo!

December 10

Written in the terrifying castle of Rattentempel. Crossing the antiquated drawbridge was a truly heroic feat on my part. But the tower — I didn't dare look at it even from afar . . . Yet tomorrow! tomorrow I must have certainty, come what may.

December 11

In the end I didn't have the courage. But it's all right: it was Friday, and the sun was not shining. Tomorrow, without fail!

If only I could take at least a small child with me — —

Again, nothing. And I knew that I wouldn't pull it off. I resolved that by tomorrow I would leave the castle. Yet in the end the whole affair shall somehow turn out well.

In the afternoon I went to the castle's small washroom to bathe. I am certain that besides me, the tub, and the lamp there was nothing there. I was rubbing my eyes, as some water had gotten in them — when suddenly something flickered in front of the tub — I looked sharply — the Daemoness was standing there, quite palpable, white, ghastly. I fainted. Having come back to my senses, I saw her no more, but I noticed that the bar on the door was bolted from within. — —

Now it is definite that it was a spook. I don't have to keep going there. That's a relief. But for God's sake, how could that spook from the washroom go cackling away at noon on the promenade with a dandy?

No, no, now it is more imperative than ever before that I go and make sure. I have a simple choice: the tower — or death in madness.

From fear of the latter, I prayed to myself: invest me with the pluck to overcome my fear of the former.

Oh, the blessings of bravery! Now as I write this I am calm, although the wind is raging so threateningly that I'm shaking like a leaf. But why be afraid? I have stationed armed servants in both the rooms next to mine; they'd show her! Well, then:

It was frightful, but I have found the greatest treasure: certainty.

Yet I would hardly have found the courage if I had not hit upon an excellent idea: to take my two enormous, trustworthy St. Bernards with me.

At two o'clock in the afternoon, having overcome the temptation to put the matter off until tomorrow, they accompanied me into the castle tower. Looking over every corner carefully, I went up to the top and then came back down again. When I passed a certain spot, both the first and the second time, it's a wonder I didn't fall, although I was aflame with bravery.

The tower staircase is divided into three sections by two iron doors. The lower door is at the height of the second story of the castle, to which the tower is adjoined. The upper one is at the height of the crest of the castle roof. Coming down the stairs, I first locked the upper door, and then the lower one, so the middle section was completely safe from potential intruders. All the same, in my wise cautiousness, I examined them yet again as thoroughly as I could before shutting the lower door, looking behind every spiderweb to see if there weren't perhaps some underhanded spy hidden there.

I returned to the castle, having locked the doors to the tower good and tight, and slowly went up to the second story. My fear grew stronger. In one of the rooms I knelt and prayed for a long time. Then, burning with stoutheartedness, I reached the room neighboring the tower, an awfully dark blue in color. There my courage left me again. Not even my prayers could bring it back. But my plucky self-mastery and the fear of going mad finally led me to action. Locking the door into the blue room, I shifted one cabinet aside, pressed the eyes of the knight painted on the wall behind it — and a secret door opened . . . I growled to the dogs: Sic him, Elephant! Get him, Lion! and ran behind them along the small corridor, shouting "heil, heil," and singing: "Es braust ein Ruf!" Then I was standing in the tower again — in the second, hermetically sealed section — having already opened the second secret door leading into it.

Once again I looked the staircase over thoroughly, and even drove away the doves sitting on the ledge — only a lunatic would have trusted them.

I stopped on a small landing, five steps higher. After praying once more, I ran my hands along the walls. At this point I noticed that one dove had flown back down onto the ledge. I went to drive it away. Again I reached for the wall — at that very moment I spotted some refuse a short distance away. I swept it into the corner with my boot — suddenly my sight went dark and I sat down. For at least a quarter of an hour I sat on the landing — oh, God! save me from hell! after all, I've already been there — and eternally! for every second was an eternity.

But the little doggies barked so happily, so happily shone the low but bright sun, that I plucked up my courage. I think that Elephant, being impatient, pulled me off to the wall by my coat-tail. And not even knowing how it happened, I pressed four bumps — and a new secret door sprang open.

Having lit the lantern, I went inside. A meter in front of me lay a small, reddish, iron door. I wanted to open it, when I smelled something awful . . . I jumped back into the stairwell . . . I was half-dazed. And that was the reason why just then, taking as deep a breath as I could, I unlocked the small, reddish door as quick as lightning, now no longer at all afraid, as I had been, that Helga would suddenly jump on my neck, or at least give a mad laugh out of the darkness — but I knew the dogs had remained outside with their tails between their legs.

An area 4 meters long and 2 meters wide lay dark before me; I boldly cast a searching glance inside.

And after a few moments of looking around, in the middle of the stone floor I saw two large, colored spots: a rose one and a green one.

On the nineteenth of August, she was wearing a green skirt and a rose blouse — — —

Silently, without moving, they lay next to one another. Silently, without moving, I gazed at them, like them a corpse . . . Then I was forced to exhale. A ghastly smell! . . .

I made it out to the stairwell on all fours, although it was possible to go out upright, and breathed deeply. Elephant and Lion greeted me with joyful barking and by fawning on me as frantically as if I were returning to them after several months' absence. Getting a hold of myself, I locked the little door coolly and collectedly, although almost without consciousness.

And then a powerful surge of delight rolled over me such as I had never felt before! After all, I had daringly accomplished what I wanted to — and acquired Certainty! . . . True, it hurt me terribly that she was dead all the same — but it was certainly much more sensible this way than if she were alive. And I didn't have to be afraid of her spook, *I was not going to be afraid of it!* My horror alone had given it life, it alone had made her dangerous, it alone could kill me . . . Oh, my plucky ancestors, invest me evermore with at least a drop of your strength into the withered veins of this modern aristocrat! . . .

On leaving the tower, I ordered that the poor dogs, who had served me so well, be shot. I wept watching their execution, but what was there to do? Their snouts could have given me away. —

It's now midnight, but there's still that ghastly smell — as if I were still standing there, in the dungeon . . . Horrors! is it possible that her graceful body, whose scent — — — But better not to think of that lest those horrible dreams revisit me.

December 14

That horrible night! Not for eternal paradise would I endure it again! Which was more dreadful, its dreams or insomnia? . . . Oh, Helga, my grisly star, whom only now, having murdered you, do I truly love — what you must have suffered! How base, eternally damnable was my deed! Yet could I have acted otherwise? Could a husband act otherwise who has seen and heard what I? . . . And then again — after all, I was merely the instrument of God, punishing a terrible sinner: is it just, Lord, that you chastise the poor instrument of your punishment so mercilessly? . . .

Well then, today I am finally making my confession on paper; at least that affords me some relief, given how much I've suffered having had to bear the burden of this terrible secret alone.

Since that afternoon when I was witness to Her scandalous rendezvous with him, my head had been spinning day and night with a wrath and a hunger for vengeance that are unimaginable.

I would never have believed before then that one could be so overwhelmed by a passion, depriving him of all self-control, sensibility, and his natural qualities; above all, it completely deprived me of fear, toward which I sometimes have a slight tendency, although at bottom I have the heart of a lion. This is the only way it could have happened that I decided to do away with Helga, and on the very day that she said would be the most beautiful day of her life. Just you wait, you bitch, I'll show you what beautiful is! And I thought up a most sophisticated plan, down to the smallest details. For four whole days I had not the slightest doubt that I would carry it out.

I avoided her. Several times, however, she sought me out on her own and began to speak to me very kindly. But in a voice as if someone were strangling her, and with a face as if she were swallowing spiders. Each time, she interrupted her speech quite suddenly and, paling, skulked off. Once, immediately afterward, I heard her hiss: "No, I can't! I can do anything, only not this . . . —"

On the nineteenth of August, from the early morning, she was very agitated, but only with a joyous, exuberant expectation. I was determined to step up to the deed as soon as I observed her preparing for her departure. But the whole morning, nothing. And only now did I waver and feel a little afraid. And the fear quickly grew stronger. I think it would never have come to the act if fate, by a peculiar dispensation, had not wished it . . .

At 2 in the afternoon, with a heavy hammer hidden under my overcoat, I looked into her room through the keyhole. She was laying various things into a small suitcase, singing softly to herself. "It's got to be now, without delay!" I declared to myself — — and at that moment I felt incapable; the terrible wrath of the last few days had now left me completely. In spite of that, I kept peering away, mechanically. She was laying out a variety of trifles, not only photographs, books, manuscripts, but also, who would have believed it, a few small, ordinary rocks, an empty, ordinary spool, an old knife handle with no blade . . . And, rummaging through a drawer, she pulled out a very precious bracelet, glittering like a rainbow with every possible stone, which I had once given her on her birthday with my own hand. She shuddered as if she were touching a scabby toad, and with all her strength she flung the jewelry into the corner, and it broke in two. And then — she carefully washed her hands.

My boundless wrath of the last few days revived and virtually propelled me inside.

Although I made a racket as I entered, she didn't even look around, now smiling again blissfully at her little spools and rocks.

"What are you doing there?" I asked after a long while, standing at a distance and leaning against a wall.

"Wha-aat?" she yawned, not even turning around, with the greatest absent-mindedness. "Wha-aat?"

"Yes — what are you doing?" I asked again in a weak voice; for her satanic presence always somehow disarmed me by its mystical power. "Well, I just dropped in, that's all — that kind of thing . . ."

Only now did she look, only now did she realize that it was I — the avenger of offended marital honor . . . But do you think the rotten creature feared or repented? . . . She roared:

"And what are you doing here? Scram!"

"I — just — — I only wanted to tell you that it's very warm outside today," I replied, my teeth chattering. But it was just a pretense on my part, you'll see in no time how I acquitted myself! . . .

"You stupid beast!" she howled, "get outside, you, or —"

Yet suddenly her hand, thrust out toward my face, dropped. She paled. And I heard the whisper: "Ah — ah! It is necessary . . . ; now or never." So then —:

"My dear husband," she commenced in a firm voice, but she shuddered; "it is well that you have come. For-give . . . me — for everything I have of-fend-ed you by . . ." She was struggling for breath, great drops of sweat burst out on her forehead. "I shall always — remember you — with the greatest af-fect-ion — —"

She could not finish. She covered her face and collapsed onto the divan as if she were made of wood . . . With extreme self-control she got out the words "You, Helmut — ohh! Come to me!" and unfolded her arms a little too . . .

I knew why she was doing all this: it was what that ragamuf-fin had commanded. But in spite of this, I approached her, slowly, cautiously, as always; thus does one approach a lioness he wants to pet . . . My rage again left me. My head was spinning with the words "Just kiss me, kiss me for half a minute and I will for-give you everything!; even if at the order of that scoundrel — about whom I have already telegraphed Willy, to have him arrested — a half-minute of your kissing — and we will be reconciled! Then go off to the Cordilleras or wherever you want, but you will return to me after you understand that you shall not find a kinder man in the world . . . I have showered you with all manner of riches, cured you of your silliness — I shall slave for you even after you return — you cannot continue to prefer such a vagabond to me. I shall not grudge him to you for now; I shall send money to the Cordilleras so that those birds of yours there will not have to sustain you!"

With such sweet, conciliatory feelings did I favor her — even now I weep for myself when recalling it. She had her fate in her hands . . .

"My little Helga," I whispered . . .

"Yours?" she let fly suddenly, roaring like a tiger. "And how is it that your stench-filled gob dares to take my name in vain?" . . .

I lurched forward — but then she fell on the floor. And I heard her moaning: "Impossible . . . Or is it? — Oh, darling, give me strength! . . . I stand — you are right — at the most terrible of all crossroads: either I — or that white, formless apparition — which is perhaps — Self . . . Lethal revulsion here — Your Will there —"

"I and lethal revulsion!" . . . An infernal rage again arose within me. Involuntarily I reached for my overcoat to see if the hammer was still there. She leapt away, white as a sheet, her face — the ghastly laughter of a corpse. Her whole body was quaking. In thinking back, I feel a deep sympathy for her. And she howled in an inhuman voice:

"Dear husband — a parting ki-i-iss —"

Once again my rage left my magnanimous heart. Everything within me melted delectably. And Helga embraced my shoulders — her lips were already touching mine . . . But it didn't come off. She wildly jumped off to the side —— and something came hurling out of her mouth. She had vomited. —

But not even that would have driven me to the act, her breath still intoxicated me divinely . . . However, she immediately roared in the ugliest voice:

"You pus, get out this instant, or I'll wipe you off the face of the earth! What stupid cowardice on my part, to do your bidding like a slave! Nevermore! . . . I shall be My Own, I shall remain My Own, and thus shall I triumph!"

But the boy was right after all. Pride goeth before the fall . . .

Judge, O people, but do not condemn! Now do I see: she, poor woman, could not help herself, but, poor me, neither could I. It was no use: the interests of all people and all creatures clash and mutually, irreparably destroy one another. Therefore the battle: a divine, unconcealed, all-out battle.

Having finished speaking, she raised her fist against me. Completely dazed at first, I took to my heels. She didn't pursue me but sat down at the table, her back turned toward me, and covered her face with her hands. I opened the door. And within me at that moment Rage again blazed hot, more savage than ever before, and now surprisingly clear-sighted. I closed the door loudly, but remained in the room. She, knowing I had always fled at her command in the past, thought that I was in the hallway.

Taking out my hammer, not trembling in the least now, I tip-toed back to her —— and without giving it a second thought, I struck her on the skull. Not too hard. Wavering on the chair, she turned her head without a word and reached into her bosom for her revolver. But before she pulled it out, the hammer fell a second time, and even harder. She collapsed and remained motionless.

Coldbloodedly, I locked the door, bound up Helga's arms and legs firmly and carefully with ropes I had ready in my pockets, stuffed her mouth full, and dragged the limp mass through several rooms into the blue one. From there I pulled her inside the tower and into — the dungeon. At that moment the sun, which had been shining relentlessly for many days, suddenly went behind a dark cloud, accompanied by booming thunder.

Since the Middle Ages my ancestors have had a lovely little place here, where their enemies would safely expire over weeks — over months — depending on whether they felt like at times throwing them a piece of rotten dog meat or a few rats, or if they spared them a jug of cow's piss. In the tower, which was built to withstand not only catapults and helepoles but also the primitive cannonades of centuries past, my grandfather once said that he had dug twenty skulls out of it with his own hands. That this cell existed was an absolute secret to everyone except the lords of the castle.

I sat down near her. A lantern shed its light upon us. The thunder's roar was muted here. The rage evaporated from my aristocratic heart, and once again everything within me was thawing; and I began to think that now I could forgive her everything . . . In spite of this I took out a 16-strap whip that I had prepared to flog her with, but I was incapable of doing this to a body that was unmoving — perhaps even dead?

"Maybe she isn't alive!" I said to myself suddenly in fear. Until now it had not even occurred to me that I could have killed her with my hammer. In my plan, it was only to knock her out so she wouldn't up and die so quickly or easily, just like that, and like a madman I believed that she merely must be unconscious . . .

I leaned over her. Her heart was beating. Weakly. The thunder was roaring.

I cannot say what was going on within me at this moment. Automatically — although this was in my plan — I attempted to — —. It didn't come off. I didn't dare unbind her legs . . . she could kill me even with her arms bound —.

But it seems that my efforts brought her to life. She stirred — and opened her eyes. Then she closed them again; for a long time. Apparently, she was thinking; she was breathing sharply. Suddenly she started to thrash about frantically — twisting for a long time like a snake over a fire. Blood dripped from her wrists. I was dying of fear that she would free herself; I stood up and backed away until I reached the door. But her exertions were in vain. When I decide to do something, I don't mess around.

She calmed back down and remained so for quite a while. Then suddenly, she said in a different voice:

"Where am I?"

"Somewhere you'll never escape from! except on the day of judgment! You're in the castle dungeon! You sinful woman, you utterly depraved adulteress! I know everything! This 'mangy dog' of yours saw and heard everything!"

She was silent. Then she was moved to speak calmly:

"I am, sir, in your power. Let's speak rationally. If you leave me here to die, you shall be destroying yourself. Your conscience is not strong enough to bear something like this for the rest of your life. I know you, and I know that even if you have a mind to release me, you are afraid that I shall take revenge for what you have done. Well, I give my solemn word that there is no need for you to fear. I am not vindictive, quite the contrary. By your act you have risen in my estimation . . . I'd like to do something nice for you in return . . . I also know that you are not vindictive either; that your moods change quickly. If you are angry at me today, you will no longer be so tomorrow. I recognize that I have always hurt you a great deal. I have deserved this humiliation. I deserve a still greater punishment — for I have not done what I intended. I see your whip next to you; well, use it, good and hard, here and now, although my head hurts terribly from your blows . . ."

I reeled sharply. She was right — even at that moment I felt that my conscience would not bear the burden of my act. But could I take her at her solemn word? The word of a diabolic individual, recognizing no moral laws whatsoever, proclaiming: I have given my solemn word to another, but not to myself. What won't a person do, especially one like this, to escape death, especially one so terrible? No! To release her would mean signing my own death warrant.

"Impossible," I replied. "You have sinned against me, God, and all people excessively. It is not I who punish you, but God."

"No, just admit that you are afraid! I swear that it is groundless, do you hear? I will leave you forever, you shall never hear of me again . . ."

"With that guy of yours, that ragamuffin?" The anger stirred within me once again; I got up to leave. And at that moment she began to plead, to flatter, even to be tender toward me. But what self-restraint I saw on her face during this! "You're acting on that lout's orders! But it's too late!" I screamed. She even made herself weep and tried to get down on her knees, but she kept falling over . . . "For heaven's sake, I beg you, at least let me have my life! Do with me as you wish otherwise — if you wish, I'll remain in your house, I'll be your slave, I'll even fulfill — — my marital obligations! It will be so awful to die, here, in this darkness and sepulchral, musty air, tied up — and after weeks of hunger and thirst! Yet I would not fear even such a death as this if I were prepared. But now, when I am just beginning to learn, to see, to live, when the gates of all the mysteries are opening before me as perhaps never to anyone else before — no, no, it's impossible! How could I die now, when I still don't even know if I am immortal! . . ."

Precious little kept me from undoing her bonds — but I suddenly, clearly sensed that the first thing she would do would be to strangle me. With extreme self-control I opened the door. And at this point her true character showed itself in all its nakedness.

"Have me untied this instant, you mangy cur!" she screamed, thinking that even now her vulgar and authoritative tone would overpower me the way it used to. "I command it! If not, I have ways of which you have not the slightest inkling to help myself — and then woe to you, woe, you rapscallion! I am in league with Satan himself — and people will know right away I'm missing and come find me! Especially my man, just you wait till he gets here! This instant, you brazen slave, the lowest of all people, the most repulsive of the repulsive!"

But this time she was grossly mistaken, and that decided her fate, as shall be seen. As I was leaving, in the depths of my soul I had darkly resolved that, postponing the matter until later, I would certainly release her in the next few days. But now my dwindled rage was again whirling within me, more terrible than ever before, and it transformed me into a savage beast, clouded my senses. I only dimly recall what followed. Having stripped the lower half of her body bare, I whipped her mercilessly. At first she endured it without a sound, without moving, and then she began to roll around the floor, finally to scream. But at the same time she cursed constantly, and still I kept it up until she fainted, completely draped in blood. And then — — I defecated onto her face; wiping it with my sock, I stuffed it into her mouth. I also spat on her a bit and blew my nose onto her face. Kicking her motionless body aside, I exited and locked the door behind me.

All this was not quite, in the fullest sense of the word, gentlemanly or gallant. But it was vital to show her that I was not a "mangy dog." — —

December 15

Dante's pen would be incapable of describing what I suffered over the following dreadful 14 days. I shall therefore be as concise as possible.

I am certain now that I would have released her on the very next day if it had not come to this last thing . . . The hope that Helga would not avenge herself upon me would have vanquished my fear. But after my last — procedure — that hope was no longer there. I had burnt all my bridges behind me, my spouse was irrevocably condemned to death. Nonetheless, for the first few days I wavered incessantly, though each time the sun set I said to myself: Yet again, if possible, there is still less hope that she would forgive me for her ever longer and more horrible agony. Every second buried her deeper and deeper . . .

Several times a day I went into the tower, and after opening the first small, secret door, I listened. There was always a rustling, a wailing, groaning murmur through her nose — oh, how gruesome! And in my hallucinatory state I heard it even in the castle, on my walks, everywhere, everywhere.

On the fourth day, the twenty-third of August, these sounds were more frightening than they had ever been . . . Barely able to stagger back into the safety of the castle, I decided to leave this awful place and depart for Berlin that very day. But this did not come to pass just yet, as a result of a terrible event of which I'll tell tomorrow —

On the twenty-fourth of August I arrived in Berlin; but not even there did I escape those terrible sounds, those terrible thoughts. They haunted me even in the clattering of wine glasses, in the laughter of the girls who embraced me, in the swishing of hundreds of dancing legs, in the blare of the music. I was experiencing Helga's sufferings down to the smallest particulars, perhaps no less intensely than she. Oh, can you have even the faintest idea of the abyss of her suffering? . . .

I returned to the castle in ten days, utterly changed and broken —: determined to set her free, come what may, if behind the iron door I still heard signs of life. I was utterly brave, as never before, not fearing even death, as I ran headlong into the tower.

I opened the secret door and listened.

Silence. I knocked on the iron door. "Helga!"

Silence. I banged with all my strength, crying:

"Helga dearest, speak to me, I'll release you immediately! Speak to me, you can't really be dead yet, I beg you in the name of the living God!"

A silence like the grave — —

I stood there for a full hour. Then I turned back into the castle. But an hour later I was running back to the tower, knocking, screaming, pleading, weeping . . .

A most sepulchral silence —

It was over. I had come too late. At least she had come to the end of her earthly suffering. But what's in store for *me* now?

December 16

Now I come to what happened on the twenty-third of August.

The first day after casting Helga into the dungeon, I was tormented no less by pangs of conscience than by fear of her terrifying lover. — Even before August nineteenth, I had set up a watch for him and found out that less than a month previous, he had come uninvited from who knows where into a little village four hours from my castle, where he had rented from its owner a half-demolished hovel located in solitude amid the rocks and woods; no one had lived in it for many years. He established himself there right away and spoke to no one, just rambled far and wide through the countryside. What he lived on, where he was from, no one knew.

Right away on the nineteenth I gave the order that he be

captured without delay. But for the next few days there was neither sight nor sound of him.

When I returned from the tower the afternoon of August twenty-third, I was so exhausted after having spent several nights lying awake that I was overcome with sleep in my study. On my orders, two servants, armed to the teeth, kept vigil in the next room.

I dreamed of him, the ragamuffin. He was carrying me with one arm by the ear, like a rabbit. I looked at myself — and I was covered in white fur, I was a rabbit with long, long ears. And he was just like a tiger, but marching on his hind legs, incredibly tall. He carried me up the tower staircase. He entered the dungeon, put me down there, and I ran around and around, because I could smell cabbage. Then I saw ropes lying on something whitish, shapeless, motionless, but with flames whirling peacefully within itself. And the tiger cut the ropes and the whitish thing slowly stirred and now had, on the body of a dragon, the head of a seraph — Helga's beautiful, celestially luminous face. She leaned on the Tiger and they began to leave. "Throw the poor little rabbit some more!" she pleaded, like the pealing of heavenly bells. And the Tiger threw me a clump of greens. "Your last meal!" he said. The doors closed behind them, and the key scraped in the lock. And with that sound, which meant, in effect, the driving of nails into my coffin, a boundless horror exploded within me — a horror of the suprametaphysical, ultra-black Grave of Eternity — and I woke up.

He was standing over my sofa. Unmoving; smiling. "I'm still dreaming," — I said to myself; "he'll catch me again by the ears

— if only he would give me clover instead of greens this time!"
I reached for my ears. No, try as I might, they were long all right,
but they weren't exactly rabbit ears . . .

His enormous figure towered high above me; slender but
strangely powerful. His tiger eyes regarded me — somehow
halfway, as if with all their strength they were stifling laughter
within themselves, and yet they were hellishly commanding —
mocking! As if this beggar, who couldn't even afford to rent a
shack that didn't leak, were the king of kings! . . . I sat up
mechanically and bleated:

"I'm just a poor rabbit, yi, yi! You won't box my ears, will you?
yi, yi!"

"What's happened to Helga?" he asked, calmly.

"To Helga? What Helga? I don't know any Helga . . . I'm
just a poor rabbit!" I gabbled, half-dreaming till now, although
my blood had slowly begun to chill.

"What's happened to Helga? Out with it!" he exclaimed, his
voice a Roman tuba.

If I hadn't been half-dreaming, he would have gotten such
a slap for the impudence of calling my lawful wife by her
Christian name alone that he'd have had a buzz in his noggin for
the rest of his life. So I just responded with:

"I — don't know — I don't know anything —"

"What's happened to Helga?" he spoke a third time. But if I
write "spoke," how incorrect it is! Only a person can speak. But
it sounded, without exaggeration, utterly, utterly like the roar of
a lion's gullet — of which my dear Prince S. once said in the zoological garden: "if one could learn from animals all their tricks,

one's pitiful little windpipe still couldn't produce even a laughable imitation of a lion's booming roar . . ." "What's happened to Helga? If you don't answer immediately, there won't be time for even one word to squeeze itself out of your throat!" And he touched, very slightly, my neck with the splayed fingers of his terrible fist . . .

"She's — in — the tow– —" I managed to eke out . . . And at that moment I would have told all, I would have led him into the dungeon . . . Oh — how good it probably would have been for everyone! . . . But fate had something different in mind for me, for him — for Her!

Terrible cries rang out. During this entire time, the two St. Bernards, of whom I've already written, had been lying in the corner behind a screen. He did not see them; and I, drowsy, had forgotten about them. No better specimens on this earth! Lion, a little smaller but still weighing more than a ton, was more fiery than Elephant, who was rather clumsy. These animals almost never barked; they thought it beneath their dignity. But anyone, without exception, who would have dared to come within less than one meter of me — would have instantly become the son of death!

They had been peaceful all this time, but when the ragamuffin raised his hand to my throat — Sic 'em! First Lion pounced on him with a terrifying, lionly leap. Yet then — — the ragamuffin staggered only slightly beneath the fearful blow. His face was all cut up, but swift as an arrow, seizing the colossus by the throat with his left hand, he swung his right one at his skull. And Lion, who had once torn apart three Gypsies who'd attacked him, lay on his back, without a sound, with only a fading tremble in his dear little legs. But at that moment Elephant, the largest dog in the world, fell upon that scoundrel. This time the blackguard took a tumble, and the blood flowed from an open cut on his shoulder. But suddenly — a miracle — Elephant flew off into the corner! The ragamuffin stood up quick as lightning — and he and the dog hurled themselves at each other all at once. And Elephant, picked up by the throat, his back pressed to the scoundrel's chest, a rattle in his gullet, shuddered so awfully that it would have sent three men tumbling. But this son of evil, not even thrown off-balance, carried him to the window and said with no loss of breath, almost tenderly:

"Forgive me, sweetheart, for squeezing your dear little neck; but since you're a dimwit it can't be helped. I hope you won't be so clumsy as to bruise your legs, but after all, this is only one story up!"

Then, having stood up, he gave the animal a little kiss on the snout, beneath which, foaming with blood, horrid fangs snapped wildly at his face. He then threw Elephant out the window.

Only now did I get a hold of myself and fled the room, screaming. On the threshold, I fell into the arms of the throng of my faithful servants, who upon hearing the noise of the St. Bernards had come rushing to my aid. I also saw the rogue, dazed as he probably was by his struggle with the animals, retreat into an adjoining room with no other exit, the windows of which were thickly barred, catch one of the servants who had torn after him around the midsection and, holding him horizontally, use him to overwhelm all the others, shoving them out and locking the doors behind them. Then I lost consciousness.

I regained it in my bedroom about two hours later. As if in a dream I heard an awful din, the cries of a hundred voices, rifle shots. Then a delectable unconsciousness again embraced me.

Only on the following day did I find out how the whole episode ended.

The ragamuffin — who, by the way, before he turned up over my sleeping self, had knocked out both my servant-guards with blows from his fists, one of them so radically that his skull busted apart like a clay pot — had remained in the room with no exit. Though he strained at the window bars, and loosened them, not even his strength could break them. He lay on the floor and smoked his pipe. My servants heard him muttering behind the door:

"You little Daemoness, you're dead. For certain, I feel it. It was to be expected. And that's all right. The devil take everything! Me? . . . I won't get out of here scot-free, that's almost certain. And what if I did? I wouldn't even want to. I love you a little more than I should. Everything here is rot. You — you are there — White. Perhaps you *are* even more than I . . . That's why you're pulling me down along with you . . . The undertaking of a life-time? Slavishness to believe in it. To You, My Only One! . . . But I promise I'll still prepare a beautiful memorial service for You — · —"

Having recognized what sort of villain they had to contend with, my servants sent into all the nearby villages for the gendarmerie and the police. Within two hours there were eight armed troops and I don't know how many constables here. And with them a host of armed villagers.

At five in the afternoon — at the hour Helga had been cast into the dungeon, they opened their attack. They tore the door apart with their axes.

Only now did the ragamuffin put his pipe aside. But in no time a heavy oak table went flying into the cluster of troops, marching forward with their bayonets poised, with such force that the skull of the first of them was shattered into smithereens. The others went rolling in a ball. And the monster hurled himself forward, clutching the heavy brass curtain rod in his right hand.

It swung so quickly that not even its golden flash was visible. Skulls cracked, brains splattered. One of the policemen was impaled by the rod, thick and round as it was, from his throat to his spine.

He worked his way through both rooms; and he found himself in the corridor, also filled to overflowing with armed men. But even here, he moved inexorably forward. Everything made way before him, more before his bestial face than before the curtain rod — a total of 18 dead and many more wounded fell victim to him that day. He elbowed his way to the window in the corridor. He jumped out. He ran through the courtyard. Shots rang out behind him. With an incredible leap he vaulted up onto the high wall. But there he staggered. He did not jump down onto the other side, but lay on his stomach, clutching his chest and twitching. My defenders converged upon him guardedly. "Nearer to You, O Daemoness!" they heard. "Eternity — Nothing — endless Beauty — — how interesting it all is — marvelously funny — — ha ha ha!" — With a laugh, the wretch croaked. — But his death deepened my resolution that the Daemoness must die. If she knew that he'd bitten the dust here — oh! no lioness pursuing those who had shot her mate and kidnapped her young could be more terrible; and it's said that nothing on this earth is more frightening.

I breathed a sigh of relief. But may God, who gave you great physical strength but simply no morals or character, be merciful even to you, you cowardly scamp.

He was buried on the carrion heap. Fortunately, Elephant and Lion remained alive and well.

•

December 20

I am living again in my chateau, Saustein, near which I caught sight of Her spirit in the woods. The chateau is cheerful, on an inviting plain, unlike the castle, situated in those terrible mountains. I always used to be happy here. And now — now — ohhh!

In vain did I look forward to the positive influence certainty would have on my health. — Alas, how one exaggerates, embellishes that which he sees as his only hope, his salvation! One always paints the supposed anchor of one's salvation in golden colors! . . . I am no longer vacillating, yet how much more frightening certainty is than uncertainty! I had struck a balance between the dragon: the Daemoness, who was perhaps still alive, and the shrew: her ghost. Now I see that one moderated the other, made the other bearable; I fled from one to the other — and was none the worse for it. And now I have fallen utterly into the shrew's maw, and nothing any longer infuses me with healing doubt . . . Ohhh, there is nothing higher than doubt, uncertainty, skepticism, twilight — poetry — magic . . . Now I fear her dagger no longer — but rather something far more horrible. Alive, she could kill my body; dead — my soul — and my body as well. Before, my conscience could take heart that I was not an actual murderer. Now I feel myself to be the most infernally damned of all souls, condemned to slow torture by a demonic power — by madness, next to which all human suffering is as nothing. Now I understand it all: I killed you, Daemoness, slowly, by hunger, and you, vengeful, will kill me more slowly still, by something far more terrifying . . .

The eternal retribution of God exists. And everything that lives is *flogged to death* for its secret sin, committed in the darkness of eternity. Blessed is the one who breathes his last after the first few blows, still more blessed the one who meets his end by a single swing of the rod, thick as a beam — ideally, right after birth. But most people are condemned to be, with a most refined slowness, by seemingly harmless switches ever-so-gradually — over 20 — 40 — 70 years — flogged to death; the "harmless" part is the worst of it. — This is the way *I* now see, the way my suffering sees — the World: a slow, fatal flogging of all its creatures — délinquants — by some kind of truly vile executioner . . . God, forgive the blaspheming of a half-trampled worm . . .

The anchor of my salvation: certainty, has only pulled me deeper into my pools. Terrible pangs of conscience, abysmal, monstrous pains, above all, desperation — night, night, night. That's what I have from my hard-won certainty. But most of all: fear of Her spirit . . . I see her always, always, until it drives me mad, always! Only her, only her! only her soiled face, an awful rag between her lips, beautiful, ethereal . . . ; I hear nothing but the endless death-rattle of someone being choked . . . lasting for whole weeks — I would go mad if I were to tell more . . . I — I — am a good person after all — did I have to commit such a deed? . . . My Lord, my Lord!

It seems to me that her constant presence in my imagination must render her ever-present in my eyes as well . . . That the horror of her *must* ultimately give birth to the *real* her! For all that is "real" is, I think, nothing but the child of imagination, of dreams . . . But I cannot say what this thought sets whirling within me, and the most ingenious philosopher could hardly even suggest what it means.

December 22

The day of the solstice; truly the greatest and only festival of the year — the festival of the Rebirth of Nature; the true New Year. I make a point of observing it; and I always make my prophecies for the entire coming year according to what happens on this day.

And this is what happened today. Having lunched in company, I caught sight of something strange in the corner of the dining hall behind the tile stove. I stood up and went to have a look. The day was dim; in the room it was as five in the afternoon, although it was only half past one. I leaned in over the thing. I saw — Her head; severed from her body; arms sticking out of the stump of her neck, like those of a cephalopod. Her face was a mess; and at the same time, it was rotted through, her cheekbones already protruding through her skin; her translucent eyes were glazed over, like those of a rotting carp. In her mouth, a sock covered in filth. On her arms, covered in blood, ropes. My blood froze. And at that moment her arms stirred, encircled me, pulled me toward her ghastly head. I fainted.

My fellow diners, having seen me fall, carried me to a sofa and revived me. Of course, none of them had seen a thing.

What does this New Year's vision of mine bode for the coming year? . . . —

December 25

Yesterday evening I was looking at the starry, icy sky, a little tree with candles burning behind me. The stars were crystals of snow. The bells tolled as though for the Last Judgment. I thought of the coming of the Savior. O Savior, will a savior come for me as well? . . . Suddenly, seized by a mysterious horror, I thought: what if she appeared now, now on the other side of the window, her face? . . . I jumped away from the window — but it was too late: her face showed terribly white beyond the windowpane, white as the snow, as the snowy stars in the firmament — her forehead pressed against the glass — her eyes . . .

O Savior, Savior, what are you planning to do with me? . . .

I shall go mad, I shall certainly go completely mad . . . In writing this, I find myself entangled in an alarming confusion of ideas — — —

December 27

My only hope is Dr. Habebald Wechselbalg, the most celebrated psychopathologist in the German Empire, with his practice in Berlin. I shall pay him a visit tomorrow.

Yesterday I went to the house of the great man. Incognito. In a simple, shabby outfit. I probably gave — because my legs made something of an X — the impression of a baker's helper. Of course, I couldn't tell this scientist about the Daemoness. I made up a story: that my dead friend, whom I had once slapped, now haunted me constantly.

I must admit that my heart was pounding when I knocked on that famous man's door.

I saw before me something like a little boy. A body — round like a clod of earth; a face — well, something so vulgar, degenerate, cretinous, can't be taken in all at once. Upon my soul, if I ever saw such a visage on any person on the street, I would stop and stare at him. But this was — a genius . . . Besides, I had often observed that so-called geniuses normally looked so disgraceful, so ridiculous, shabby, wretched, like garbage, like rejects, the dregs of humanity. The fact that this is how Dr. Wechselbalg looked only increased my respect for his mind.

He eyed me, rather my clothing, and on his face appeared an expression of the greatest indignation. "Whatcha want?" he rattled out.

I replied that I had come for a consultation. "Be quick about it then, time'zmunny! D'ya got any?"

I showed him a few larger banknotes. He muttered more welcomingly:

"So speak then, be quick about it! Time'zmunny, don't think I'll letcha rob me! Spill it, all of it, straight out!"

"'Straight out,' that's what you think!" I said to myself, "If all the advice you give me is as wise as this, there was no point in my coming to see you." But he didn't mean the part about "all of it" seriously. And I said:

"I had a friend, a maltster in a brewery, and he died. I once slapped him a couple of times, and he —"

"I know already, I know all 'bout it. Waitaminnit. Hallucinations. That's easy. Don'eat'ny meat, no spices, just beans, veg'bles an' milk. Don't smoke and don't drink anything 'cept this soda water I've 'scovered and manufacture, it nev' fails. Spend lotsa time outdoors, lotsa cold baths — and 'sides that be hap', plucky, and calm all the time, don't work mental, at least three hours' hard phyz'cal layb'raday — and take this med'sin, no more than a half-t'spoon daily, lissen, no more, else — catastrophe. And I'll take 50 f'th'consultation, 30 marks f'th'med'sin."

I was in heaven — such self-confidence, confidence in his worth, demanding such handsome remuneration, had a hypnotic effect on me. — "When will I feel better?" I asked again, paying . . .

"In a week. And f'th'reply I'll take 'nother tenner."

I hardly had time to whoop for joy before I found myself outside again.

January 7

I followed the professor's instructions with the utmost care. I lived on only vegetables, beans, and milk; yet inasmuch as these things had never agreed with me, it upset my stomach. I imbibed only that soda water of his, which of course "did not fail" to work: I had diarrhea like Diana, so that only crystalline water came out of me. I forswore smoking, which used to give me some relaxation, and I now felt constantly ill at ease, bored, depressed. I drank nothing alcoholic and now had not even a single bearable moment, whereas before, when I had gotten thoroughly drunk, at least for a few hours I felt good, happy, and plucky. As for not doing any mental work — there was really no need to advise an aristocrat not to do that! For three hours a day I dug and delved, etc.; the result of all this was that every part of me, down to my unaccustomed limbs, ached so badly that I couldn't even get out of bed. I also endeavored to be happy, plucky, and calm; pity that the great mind had forgotten to give me a prescription for attaining this; he had taken the means to calm, happiness, and pluckiness — nicotine and alcohol — away from me, that thief, and given me nothing to replace them. — I took the medicine, also according to orders, but I could observe no effect. Until today, just as the professor forecast! Putting myself to bed, when I pulled away the duvet, I saw beneath it a human skeleton, and bound to it by a cord, intact, the laughing face of the Daemoness . . .

I am writing, unable to fall asleep. Perhaps I have written what has happened up to now sensibly enough . . . But do not believe it. I am a madman . . . When I beheld — this thing, it was as if something crumpled in my brain. At another time, I might have been able to bear the sight; but today, as a result of the regimen of the last few days, my organism is disturbed, exhausted, with little resistance left . . . I walked around a little on all fours, saying constantly "hoo, boo, hoo hoo boo"; — taking my slipper on my lap, I caressed it for a long time, telling it: "Num num num, you're my little black kittycat, aren't you?" . . .

I have not sufficiently followed the psychopathologist's advice. I'll make up for it tomorrow —

Num num num — — —

January 8, evening

First thing in the morning I ordered that a cauldron — the one in which they cook for the 40 swine being raised on the chateau's grounds — filled with beans, cabbage, carrots, onions, garlic, absolutely every possible vegetable in the world, all cooked in milk and Wechselbalg Soda Water, be prepared for me. Inasmuch as he had ordered me to take cold baths and to spend all my time outdoors, I commanded that a bathtub of ice water be brought to me in the garden. And in order to exercise my body, I had a heap of logs and a saw brought to me. When they brought the cauldron, I got into the bathtub and fed on the beans and carrots and parsley like a goat and drank green milk and Wechselbalgian solution from the cauldron. I was puking like a dog, but nevertheless I sawed logs heroically, and in order that I be happy and plucky according to instructions, I yelled: hip, hip, hooray! no one scares me today; and in order that I be calm, I resolved to imitate the English: I put on a monocle, breezily hissed to myself over and over again "all right" and spluttered through my teeth. As for alcohol and nicotine, I abstained from them completely for an entire week, but in order to increase my enmity toward both poisons, I had cases of cigars and a battery of bottles of absinthe brought, and with a battle cry I smashed it all to pieces.

The servants did not dare to intervene by themselves. They called Berlin for my aunt. After I had spent two hours in bath water yellow from my excrement, she arrived in her automobile and punched me in the head several times, whereupon the servants bore me away to bed, half-dead from the violence.

Luckily it was 8 degrees above zero on the Réaumur scale that day.

It is midnight. Oh, what difficult work it was to write down these few lines! I am a lunatic . . . Hoo hoo, boo boo boo . . . But I shall not remain a lunatic, I can feel it! This heroic day has given my soul élan, and will surely help it to turn things around.

My faithful servants have been watching over me so that tomorrow they can commit me to the madhouse. Not only is my aunt here, but also a whole gaggle of my dear relatives, my heirs. But you're miscalculating, you gluttonous louts! Being of sound mind and body, I shall designate my black kittycat from yesterday as my sole heir. —

Signed
My Excellency Prince Helmut Sternenhoch
Acting Rabbit and Lunatic

January 28

As I suspected, the heroic eighth of January was very effective. I became seriously ill, and for several days I was unconscious or delirious. This eradicated the madness that had been threatening to overwhelm me. When my senses became clear again, the madness had upped and gone. But even afterward: debilitation —

lovely dreams always, and all those beautiful thoughts that accompany illness and convalescence, joy that I was getting well — all this caused me not even to think of the Daemoness. Hey! only now am I beginning to penetrate the mysteries of medical science, as Frederick the Great penetrated the secrets of strategy only after he had been thrashed. This was also the goal of the professor: that I fall seriously ill and thus become well. An ingenious idea: to defeat illness with illness; similia similibus curare.

All that matters is whether the beneficial effects of my illness will continue to last even after my health returns. For I feel that I should not survive another such treatment by illness.

February 2

My health has returned. While dozing off, I heard a scratching at the door. "That must be Elephant or Lion," I said to myself, forgetting in my drowsiness that they had gone to meet their maker. — I opened the door — She! . . . And I don't know what happened next. — It seems that she somehow violated me — —.

Little by little I shall begin to lunch with her each day —. Heh heh heh heh.

February 3

I have still not lost my faith in science. There is still that medicine. The professor strictly forbade me from taking more than a half-teaspoon. Yet inasmuch as his advice was out-and-out stupid, perhaps his caveats will turn out to be stupid as well. And thus heroically resolved, I swallowed the rest of the medicine, which was supposed to last me three more weeks.

"Tomorrow I shall wake up dead. Let me! God, let it be that I shall awaken after this earthly purgatory next to You in heaven. Ha! All my insides are convulsing, terrible pains — woe, woe is me, amen . . ."

February 4

I awoke not in heaven but in my bed. But what if this bed is in heaven? What if I'm only dreaming that I have awoken? After all, I must be dead, dead . . . And I felt so wonderfully heavenly. I had never felt so lovely; I jumped out of bed, danced and sang . . . The valet brought me breakfast: Berlin-style bread —

Oh, you psychopathological swine! . . . — Yet the whole time I felt so wonderful that I considered myself saved from the evil spirit, definitively, once and for all.

However, late in the afternoon, when I was strutting through the corridor, someone abruptly clapped a hand on my shoulder. I looked around; nothing anywhere. I lunged through the nearest doorway — Helga stood before me, offering me her hand with a curtsy and chuckling: "Looks like I caught up with you, eh? . . ."

February 6

Science has let me down. I have decided to take refuge in superstition. There is a celebrated sorceress by the name of Esmeralda Carmen Kuhmist, the daughter of a pastor and a Gypsy woman, who lives in Berlin. They say she performs every kind of miracle possible. I shall go there this very day.

Well, I went to see her. Again incognito, a scruffy baker's helper. I saw a woman who was 45 years old, tall, with a classical, austere, downright majestic face; what a contrast with that stupid blockhead, Wechselbalg! I told her the story of the slapped maltster as well. "Oh, help is easy, my dear sir!" she cried, with holy conviction in her voice; "you shall be cured at once — yet — yet it will cost a great deal of money . . ." "Very much?" "Ah — 15 marks!" "That much? Sweet Jesus, where will I get it?" "Well, my dear sir — out of love for my neighbor I shall do it for 12 . . ." "Would it be possible for 10? . . ." "All right — in the name of the Lord, for 10! And now, sir, rejoice! As the sun blesses the earth, that hellish power shall lose its power over you! Omnipotent is my remedy!"

And from the cabinet she produced an ordinary nut wrapped in twine. "In this nut, your lordship, there are mysterious substances, exceedingly rare, such as are not found on our earth. Here are a viper's droppings that first saw the light of day in a pine grove in January, having been secreted onto a fern blossom. Next, the teardrop of a gorilla. Item, the sweat of a diamond before, in mortal anxiety, bursting into flame in an exceedingly wondrous heat, it fell back into the sun, its maternal womb. Finally, the crimson rays of the planet Aldebaran, captured in a glass trap. Over all of this has passed the breath of a virgin who has given birth to 13 children without a man ever touching her. However, the most important thing here is the quill of a frog, beautiful as the smile of a grown maiden, which happens only once in a century; thrice, four times blessed is he who finds it in the moment the frog sheds it and, picking it up, immediately bestows his kiss upon it; the world's greatest treasure is to be found within himself. — This wonder-working nut, which goes by the name of Podex romanus, you must wear constantly on your heart and never look inside it, lest the substances within lose their power, and you shall pay dearly indeed for your sinful curiosity and unbelief. For belief alone makes one blessed; unbelief is an absolutely destructive principle; belief is the only thing that heals, yet the professors have not the least understanding of it. — And if fear should lay hold of you in spite of this talisman, say to yourself loudly over and over again: 'Ghost, jump up my ass!' If your fear does not leave you in spite of this, shout these words louder and louder; if not even this helps, roar them until the building shakes. — You are saved, sir!"

She spoke so energetically and majestically that I came to believe with all my heart, religiously; I felt exalted in my soul. Hanging the talisman on my chest and paying a hundred marks instead of 10, I raced home, challenging all ghosts to come take me on.

March 28

Blessed art thou among women! I shall shower you with millions if my current state lasts another year! I am cured, cured! And only one who has been ill can grasp the magical significance of that word.

No knight ever felt more safe and stout-hearted beneath his armor than my heart beneath my nut. An ineffable, blissful certainty has permeated my entire soul. "Nothing can harm me ever again, nothing!" I tell myself this all the time now and believe it, and in truth nothing has harmed me. Let anyone try and come crawling to me now with his science! I'll kick him in the ass!

The first days after my visit to the wonder-working woman, my previous fright took hold of me often, of course, but whenever I took up the deafening roar: "Daemoness, jump up my ass!" — until the chateau shook and all kinds of people came running up to me, shame and then laughter always radically dispelled every fear. If she had appeared to me in this mood, I would have had, whether I wanted to or not, to laugh at her, I would have killed her with laughter! . . . Blessed art thou among women!

At the end of February my fear completely disappeared, and with it all my pangs of conscience; my memories of Helga had been extinguished. Over the next two weeks I didn't think of her at all; I basked in my happiness, ate terribly spicy meat, got drunk, smoked, didn't touch physical labor, didn't bathe, never went into the outdoors; the only thing in which I obeyed that swine was that I did no mental work.

Helga, Daemoness, jump up my ass!

March 29

May the sky come crashing down! Today I caught sight of her again, and — — I even spoke with her for a long, long time! . . . Just think, I spoke with her as if with any ordinary person! . . .

That perfidious Kuhmist! . . . But no, you can't help it, it's that lousy book; I saw Helga before I could shout out my spell . . . But was she a ghost? After all, she was as real as my gardener, who found me sitting in the mud. If it were not so certain

that her body was asleep in an eternal dream there in the tower
— —. It would drive me crazy.

I was strolling through the chateau park beneath the swelling
buds of the trees. It was morning; cloudy, warm, though damp
and windy; a balmy, blissful springtime mood all around. I was
perusing the lewd illustrations in that accursed book; and I was
so deeply absorbed in them that the blue ladies' dress on the bench
flickered into view only when it was but three paces away. I lifted
my eyes — and was suddenly sitting right in a heap of runny mud
that the gardener had raked off the path yesterday. —

"Rise, Prince!" she said, kindly.

"I don't want to, I don't want to," — I babbled like a little boy.

"Why don't you want to?"

"Because I don't want to — and because I can't."

"One can see that you are wise," she said to me, just as sweetly
and quietly. "'I want to because I want to' is summa theoretical,
yet 'I do not want to do what I cannot' is practical philosophy.
Well then, as you wish. — I have come with a request for various
explanations."

"At your service," I blurted out. —

It is a bottomless abyss of horror seeing someone whom we
had unmistakably seen dead, alive, speaking, real before our
eyes! There is simply nothing on this earth that could be so
insanely terrifying! . . . I would have fainted had my horror not
been mitigated by the surprising peacefulness and delicateness of
her voice; she had never spoken like that with me before. And that
voice was deeply sorrowful, and her face, terribly white and gaunt,
exuded infinite suffering.

"I would like to find out what happened to me on the nineteenth of August — do you remember that day? — and in the time that followed. Despite all my efforts, the blurry memories refuse to come into focus. I remember my life clearly up until that day, although it is now enveloped in a kind of alienating, estranging mist, although it feels to me like a submerged dream . . . ; but all the rest is impenetrable darkness. This makes my current state all the more paradoxical, and I think that I should overcome all my sufferings if only my soul found sufficient strength to penetrate and dissipate the unbearable mists of uncertainty with the gaze of the sun. Well then, my last clear recollection is that when I meant to begin my journey, I felt that I was losing consciousness in one of the rooms of your castle; and I know that you were present. Tell me, why did I faint?"

I twitched so violently that I found myself lying down in the mud. "I — I — don't know — — most likely because you — ate too much at lunch —"

"Let's see, that must be how it was. And what happened to me then?"

"I — I — don't know —"

"What did you do, my husband, when I fainted?"

"Aha! I ran for the doctor —"

"And when you returned?"

"I — I've forgotten —"

"I meant so little to you that you could forget such a thing?"

"Aha! You were no longer there. In the meantime you had disappeared — most likely you had left, in your semiconsciousness, through the castle park — into the neighboring forest —"

"Aye, aye! That could have happened. And apparently I sank down again in the forest — fell asleep — and all the rest is only my dream, which I have probably been dreaming for just a short time in that forest, though it seems to be lasting an eternity. And even the fact that I am now conversing with you is probably also just my dream . . ."

"Yes, it must all be just your dream!" I cried feverishly, pleased to find she believed that.

"You are not competent to decide this, being merely a product of the dream yourself — but who would get mixed up in this! To be honest, I did not come to you so much in the hope that you would tell me anything worthwhile, but to while away some time in this horrible condition of mine. If you wish, I shall tell you everything I have dreamed."

"It would please me to no end." Oh, unlucky woman!, my soul shuddered, she doesn't realize she is dead, she is narcotizing herself with the belief that she is sleeping and dreaming . . . For the idea "I am dead" is fundamentally unbearable . . . But are not we the living — dead? is this not all merely our post-obit dream? and are we not even more blind than the Daemoness? She considers her death a dream, while we, idiots, consider it wakefulness! . . .

"Well then, first I dreamed that I was lying in a small vault, with no window, lit by a lantern; around me — rotting bones. I was bound; above me, a man. I would give a great deal if I could remember what he looked like and what he said to me. I know only that he flogged me terribly, until I fainted. When I came to, there was absolute darkness all around me. Still bound, hand and foot, so tightly that I bled; a rag, smeared with feces, in my mouth; my face, nose, eyes — covered in excrement; my almost naked body, now become one single wound on the sharp stones, the sharp, rotting human bones. A black silence, darkness, the mad, droning music of time. And an ever-growing hunger, and a thirst worse than that; cold. Mad rage and hatred and vengefulness and impotence and boredom and horror of the present; horror and regret over the past; and horror of approaching death, which only now became real to my endlessly suffering soul in all its awfulness. And hopelessness, for I knew that whoever had cast me in here would leave me to perish, although there was an even greater temptation within him to release me. Yet why go on describing the indescribable? — I just kept circling round and round with a terrible effort, back and forth through the darkness, searching the walls with my dirty face for a protruding stone, that I might try to cut through my fetters on it; in vain. Oh, oh — — — But enough! After all, it was only a dream. As to how long it lasted in earthly time, I do not know; but I think it was 14 days. Finally there came a blessed peace. —

"And then, a new kind of dream; something strange. I felt myself to be without a body. But in its place, an ineffable darkness burdened my soul. An extremely oppressive, suffocating, monstrous, formless dream, but recognizably different than all that I had dreamed in the nights before the nineteenth of August. 'This is what consciousness after death might be like,' I told myself, 'if consciousness after death even exists.' I will not belabor this — —. Yet alongside its essential blackness and heaviness, it also had moments of clarity and lightness; memories of my former life, perhaps also of earlier lives, occasionally flashed intensely through its night; sometimes I saw, *in the fullest sense of the word,* places familiar to me from an earlier time, and I moved in them just as I do now, next to you; for my meeting with you was only one of the flashes in my black dream. It would not be so bad if it didn't alternate, every 24 hours with mathematical precision, with another dream —" She fell silent for a while and shuddered. My hair stood on end. "So now I am hearing, perhaps as the first person ever, something of what comes after death . . ." Although I was keen to learn more details, I lost the courage to ask. And Helga continued:

"After the end of my dream in the dark, small cellar, the dream I have just described, rambling and misty, went on for 24 hours according to earthly reckoning. Then I heard a faint but inexpressibly ghastly noise, as if a metaphysical hurricane were churning somewhere beyond the horizon. I shuddered to the depths of my soul, knowing beforehand that it was for me and that it was conveying something most horrible. It grew in strength — and suddenly I felt a wild gale lifting me, my body now somehow half-naked, and with bestial speed it carried me off somewhere. Complete darkness all around me. But in a short time I saw before me a small, crimson star. It quickly grew, acquiring a four-sided shape; finally I discerned that it consisted of innumerable crimson spots. It grew — until I saw that it was an enormous building, through the windows of which shone red flames, blazing within. The length of its facade was about 1000m, its height the same. And the hurricane swept me into one of the ground-floor windows. I found myself in a hellishly-lit room.

Horrible monsters bound me by my hair to the ceiling, and some kind of machine, equipped with about 200 strong rods, surrounding me all the way around, were set in astonishingly rapid motion. The rods lashed my body, and also my head, all at the same time; in a moment I was a bloody pulp. Did I lose consciousness, or did I die? . . . But no, I was immediately brought to myself by an enormous pair of pincers that picked me up by the neck and pulled me through the ceiling to the first floor. There they flung me — my body suddenly restored — into a chest full of bees and wasps and closed it over my head. Again they pulled me out, dead, revived me and conveyed me to the second floor, where I was put into a barrel, the interior of which dazzled with a thousand needles glowing white-hot; and the barrel began to roll rapidly . . . In the next section, my head was bound in a sack stuffed with the most disgusting insects: cockroaches, caterpillars, spiders, etc., in addition to toads and rats . . . One floor higher, the monsters tied me to the ceiling by my little toes, head downward, and then one of them began to pierce me with long needles through my nostrils, until the points dug into my brain; at the same time, a second one pulled out all my teeth with a special instrument, a third slit open my stomach, tore out the intestines, and poured a jug of molten lead into the cavity; a fourth plunged white-hot iron rods into my vagina and anus; and a fifth shattered my kneecaps with an enormous mallet; all this at the same time. I would continue to describe it, but it looks like you're about to faint on me. Briefly: I went through all 200 rooms from the floor to the roof in six hours, and then another 200 that ran the length of the roof — as the building formed a perfect cube. Then it went down again along the opposite wall, and my torments in each successive room were more cruel — it is interesting that *there* they can progress right into infinity. Finally, it continued along the length of the ground floor. And here it was the worst. No longer in the physical sense: purely mental, metaphysical horrors simply unthinkable, meant only for gods, for God . . . — Exactly 24 hours after my arrival at that inhospitable building I found myself back in the room where I had started. And the moment the monsters threw me outside, the hurricane picked me up and bore me away, by now deprived of consciousness for some time to come, into the darkness. —

"Then once again, for 24 hours, another of those bearable dreams followed — until finally the hurricane thundered anew and bore me off to the kilometer-long palace. Now it swept me into the window next to the one I had been cast into two days before — and I went through the same series of rooms upward and along the roof, etc., until I had ticked off another 800 of them. And thus it has continued to this day; in every chamber a new torment, each one more ghastly; and I am not getting tougher, on the contrary, I am becoming more and more sensitive. Since almost seven months have gone by from the beginning until today, let's say 200 days, let us multiply 800 x 100 = 80,000 little rooms. It's amusing, isn't it, Prince?" she laughed — but immediately afterward, she shuddered horribly.

"You are in hell, most unhappy Helga!" I howled from deep within myself. But I immediately became frightened. "No, no, you're only dreaming this in the forest —"

"One does not exclude the other, on the contrary: hell exists only in dreams, and dreams are by their nature only hell; nothing can exist outside dreams. But perhaps dreams are damnably real torment — ha!" She writhed like a steel spring, and such horror streamed from her face that I felt it would destroy me like the head of a Gorgon. "What kind of treatment is this for a poor woman?" she cried, bursting violently into tears. And I blubbered right along with her —

But suddenly, she drew up her courage. "Ugh! It has not broken me and it shall not! I will remain what I am, tall and proud!"

"Let yourself be broken, kneel, change!" I cried from deep within myself. "Apologize, repent! Perhaps God will forgive you, surely you are not in hell, only in purgatory . . ."

"Am I so sullied that I have need of purification? To apologize? how can I, when all I've ever done meets my approval?"

"You killed enough people, even your own child and your father!"

"Bagatelles! Everyday life is nothing but murder, the same as giving birth. Killing a person is no worse, and less so, than killing an idea. If I want to kill an idea, I can only do so by placing another, stronger, i.e., greater one in its place; what is learning? Merely killing in rebus psychisis. Similarly, if I kill a living being, then ipso I have made possible the life of another: I have freed a space where evolution will rush in by the same necessity as air into a vacuum. 'Murder': nothing more than an idiotic, utterly craven social prejudice. I do not reproach myself for having killed many people, but for having killed too few; and then again — — that I killed them from motives which were not always entirely divine . . . ; and here is the root of my evil — —. Of course, before, in the initial faintheartedness of my dream, I thought someone was punishing me for something; yet later it dawned on me that the concept of punishment did not make the least sense in regard to me, who *craves* everything horrible, because I want All, seeing in everything only My Eternal Radiance; can a God be punished? . . . Yet I would still like to know why I am now being visited by the most curious dreams . . . It is probably to prepare me, to strengthen me for the enormous tasks I have set for myself. With Him . . . But I do not see him now, ever; and that is the worst . . . However, the thought of him is all that has kept me from breaking down. Prince, you were spying on us once on the knoll, you know him, don't deny it! Can you give me any news of him?"

"I — I — know nothing, or actually I do. He's doing well. He has gotten fat, like a darling pet. And — and — he's taking better care of himself now. After all, dear Helga, it was a disgrace for you, those frayed pants of his. I'll support him, would you like that?"

"My greatest fear is that after I awaken from this dream I will be as gray as an old woman, and that he will — — Prince, how do I look?"

"Not well, truly awful; at least ten years older."

"Prince, you are an uncouth flunky!" She snapped at me, today for the first time. "Ten years older! . . ."

"I beg your pardon, I misspoke — I meant ten years younger."

"So I look like a 13-year-old, thank you kindly. You're stupid as a pig, Prince. I have no idea why I came to see you . . . If you are such a dolt as a real being, at least you could be more intelligent as a phantom in my dream. — Adieu! We shall see each other again. It would be kind of you if you managed to find out who that man in the vault was; I must settle my accounts with that gentleman who shat upon the face of a bound, unconscious woman!" She stood up to leave. "In any event, my 24 hours are coming to an end — hasn't the sound of my hurricane come yet? . . . Yes, it is already howling from afar — ohh — — ohhhh" —

Her hair stood on end, her face paled white as chalk, and she collapsed onto the wet ground with a horrible shriek. "This endless horror, how shall I bear it? Agh, is there no, *no* way for me to conquer it? Only why, why do we lose our will in our *dreams?* . . . Is it worth — anything at all, then? — It is howling ever more terribly — oh God, you cruel god, no: merciful! take this from me! hear me! grant me this! At least once, now, avert from me the crimson house — and I will swear to everything! I'll surrender my will! I shall be broken, a humble worm before your countenance! . . . It is already blowing quite close" —

She was caught up and went reeling off; and I heard her words as they faded away:

"Ohh, I know, ohh, I know what you want from me, you lily-livered, white ghost, you polyp! . . . That I yank myself out of this, like a tooth . . . That I destroy my greatest strength: my hatred and nastiness and revulsion and vengeance! . . . That's why there was the vault, because it was impossible for me to over-come my hatred — by kissing — and that's the reason for the scarlet house, because *I cannot overcome — vengefulness — by something more difficult, still more terrible* — more impossible, more impossible . . . You never, you degenerate god, lighten a person's burden, you only pile on more, and the lower he stoops, the more you add, you tormentor, tormentor — ohhhhh — it's already taking hold of me — —"

Then there was a roar more terrible than that of a tiger in the throes of death — Half-fainting, I saw her disappear in the spruce grove like a wisp of bluish mist, billowing as if buffeted by the wind — — Her outlines dissipated — or was everything fading before my eyes? She had disappeared, become mute. And I remained sitting in the mud, weeping, weeping —

Just then I felt something touch my shoulder. It was strangely as if a weight had been lifted from me. I looked awkwardly around myself — and recognized my gardener.

"On the five wounds of the Lord Christ, what is Your Excellency doing here? In a heap of mud! Oh my! If Your Excellency had been pleased to seat himself thus in July, that would have made sense, but in March? Oh my, your excellent behind shall certainly catch a chill! If Your Excellency would be pleased to come with me into the chateau, I shall kindly change Your Excellency's outfit, all muddy, muddy, how unfortunate, how unfortunate . . ."

"Did you see a lady sitting here on the bench?"

"What lady? I didn't see anything —"

"The Daemoness, you simpleton!"

"I don't know her, Your Excellency! —"

"How long have you been in the garden?"

"Well, since early morning, Your Excellency; I know my responsibilities."

"Did you at least see me here before?"

"Yes — I did see you, from a distance, something on the mud there, but I didn't know that it was pleased to be Your Excellency;

it was pleased to have a grayish outfit, like the mud there, so I thought that Your Excellency was mud. Only when I heard the mud weeping did I come running."

"Listen, you ass, did you hear a terrible roar a moment ago?"

"I did, Your Excellency. The beasts were roaring so savagely that my blood stood still. I ran to see if that rabble hadn't gobbled each other up, but it was nothing. What's more, they'd been roaring for a whole hour, God knows why; they have plenty to eat; if the likes of you or me had so much meat — —"

"So it was the beasts who were roaring?" I said, already pulled halfway home by the gardener. "So, you blockhead, you really didn't see anyone on the bench?"

"Hm, hm — to tell the truth, for a moment it seemed to me that the bench was somehow blue, and after all, it's brown. But God knows what it was, maybe it was a little bit of sky being reflected on the lacquer there —"

I really didn't find out a thing from that idiot. — But in the end — even if he had seen her blue dress and heard her howling, would that have been proof of her reality? Why couldn't more than one person have had the same vision simultaneously? Not a hallucination, of course; that would go against the concept of a hallucination as something simply empty and subjective. But it was all stupidity. The only thing that was quite certain was the fact that she was dead.

Having stripped the mud off myself, I got into bed. The strangest thoughts were going around in my head. Again it felt like my madness was coming on. But then I drank a pint of cognac; that cheered me up and calmed me, and within an hour

I was sleeping like a log. Only in the evening did I awaken — with my mind altogether stupid, yet quite recovered.

The most important thing is: my terrible horror of Helga's apparition has completely disappeared; now I almost wish she would appear to me more often. I feel only boundless compassion and tenderness toward her. No longer do I shiver to my bones with horror of her, only of her hell; — where I shall perhaps follow her, blessed God!

The other thing is, I'm afraid she'll remember that gentleman, and then come and whip me like a horse — —

March 31

The feeling that I'm no longer afraid of that ghost convinced me that I'd been liberated from it, even if Esmeralda Carmen Kuhmist's spells were no help. Now I see that I have exchanged one hell for another. While I have no fear of the ghost, or almost none, at the same time my horror of divine punishment is all that much greater; it could drive me to madness, as fear of the Specter did earlier. And I am more and more afraid that she'll suddenly attack me like a fury and give me a good thrashing. She is capable of anything.

And what's more, uncertainty is gnawing at me again . . . Comic it is — though it often feels like Helga is alive after all. Everything is somehow open to doubt. If only my gardener weren't such a dunderhead . . .

My mind keeps wondering if the soul of that condemned woman, hungry for vengeance, is not artfully leading me by the nose, if everything she told me was not merely her diabolical invention, if she isn't following some kind of hellish plan, if she is not playing with me like a tiger with a bit of human prey . . .

Apropos: those four beasts, as all the chateau personnel attest, were roaring terribly the entire time I was speaking with the Daemoness.

You must know: before, as long as she was still alive, whenever she spent time away from the chateau, those monsters were unhappy and did not roar. But when — blessed God! I cast that magnificent being into the dungeon — although they were 200 kilometers away, what did they do? For an hour's journey in every direction, the peasants were kept awake by their roaring! . . . Tears fell from those wretches' eyes — at least that's what their keepers said. — When, on the twenty-fifth of August, I fled from the castle where she was dying to Berlin, I spent the night in Saustein. I didn't get even a moment's sleep. I dreamed that a longing, desperate roaring, thirsting for the tigress's liberation, was coming directly from my bedroom. The next morning I gathered up my courage and approached their enclosure. They caught sight of me from the depths of their artificial jungle, and with a few leaps they were right in front of me. Their roaring was such that I could not hear for several days afterward. Those hellish cat-eyes — Her eyes, piercing me until I almost fainted. Their paws swiped at the enormous grillwork with such force the thick iron bars buckled like wicker. Petrified with horror, I nonetheless found the courage to run away at breakneck speed and scream for help.

God, to think what they'd have done with me if they'd gotten out! . . . They raged until the second of September. Then they were overcome by a puzzling apathy. They did not eat or roar for nearly a month; it looked like they were going to croak. But then they began to feed again; yet from that time on they were unhappy, and no one heard them roar. They only lay around and slept. They had to be thrown pieces of meat — they wouldn't have managed to kill even a lamb.

I'd rather have sold the lot of them to Hagenbeck or, better still, had them shot. They poisoned my stay in Saustein. They can't escape, yet — if only. — I would have been the first one they threw themselves on . . . The tiger loves the tigress. I've killed their Helga. — And I've also been thinking: Daemoness, if I look after your little darlings as you did, perhaps your vengeance will be less cruel.

This very day I shall write Hagenbeck: Ten rhinoceroses! But — for God's sake, now I recall: when you were still alive, you ordered a female for each of these beasts. They did not arrive, for they drowned in the ocean. I shall write Hagenbeck right away for four lionesses, item tigresses, jaguaresses, and pantheresses. — Just don't thrash me too much, dear Helga, when you find out — —. I'm a good boy, I'm a good boy.

But those beasts caught your scent the day before yesterday . . . Oh God, were you perhaps —? But — after all, they can also sense the presence of a spirit; it is well-known that animals can do that better than people. — Tomorrow I'll flee to Berlin.

April 4, Berlin

Rejoicings, revelry. But the Daemoness does not leave me even for a moment. I'm not feeling too badly though. At least my torment isn't getting worse. What does not grow, dies, however slowly. Even a goat's got to kick the bucket sometime — so say the Poles; my suffering shall also kick the bucket. — —

And perhaps it's already over. I feel so well. Hip, hip, hooray! After all, the main thing is that it no longer even occurs to me to be afraid of a ghost! And I think it won't even come back any more; it's afraid of me. Hip, hip, hooray! I'm as soused as a sponge, but that's how it ought to be! Helga, jump up my ass!

April 7

I've been feeling consistently marvelous. But I simply must finally visit dear old Willie. I've already announced my arrival to him. I don't really want to go see him. But he is so awfully fond of me. I am certainly in Disfavor; partly because it's been such a long time since I've made him happy and furthermore, because my eccentricities have certainly reached His and Augusta's ears. Of course the Imperator Rex is kept well-informed — except of what is most important.

But I don't know which would be more unpleasant for me: his disfavor or his favor.

I am continually happy and besotted. Dear Helga, you stinker, take care of things with the Lord God as best you can. I'll take care of them with the girls. Hot damn, these girls from the Berlin bars are good-lookers — —

April 10

Well, I finally made it there; in the afternoon I received a dry invitation to dinner. I was trembling as I ascended the palace steps.

The valet announced my arrival. Almost immediately the music struck up — sit venia verbo! They say it is possible to recognize every great composer by the deep, distinctive character of his music. If that is so, then Wilhelm II is surely the greatest of them all: even a person as unmusical as I can tell by the absolute unmelodiousness and unharmoniousness that it was He who "composed" it. Unmelodiousness and unharmoniousness are characteristic of all modern compositions; yet while other compositions pay no heed to melody and harmony, the emperor's compositions represent their most stunning *opposite;* whereas in other compositions there is the interplay of white and red, in the emperor's there is the interplay of white and black.

This composition was supposed to be a welcoming fanfare for little old me. The doors opened, I entered — and the music came to a halt. From the neighboring room, however, an entire operatic ensemble suddenly launched into a song that began with the words: "Hey, hey, up my ass, hey, hey, up my ass, up my ass jump!" The libretto was indisputably the monarch's mental progeny as well.

And He himself stood before me; clicking his heels together, he saluted before me, maintaining that pose majestically until two verses had been sung, observing the enchanting effect of his art. Then a commanding gesture — and the music ended. And the Imperator intoned:

"Do not think, dear Sternenhoch, that the Kaiser's long salute was for you; it was not for you, but for the art that has just delighted us. Welcome! You are late, but better late than never; although I have often lost my temper with you, you have not lost much of My Favor. As proof of this, see what my delicate consideration has prepared for you!

I looked in the direction he was gesturing and spotted a cauldron that held at least ten hectoliters, full of beans, cabbage, carrots and so forth in a whitish-green liquid. Next to it stood a bathtub full of water and next to that, a chopping block, logs, an ax, bottles, and cases full of cigars.

"Heil dir im Siegeskranz, the greatest German hero, Arminius II!" continued the monarch. "The entire contents of the cauldron are for you, and we are firmly convinced that you shall polish it off this very day! And the Kaiser asks of you, and Augusta, as is fitting for a proper wife, concurs in His request, although being jealous of you she does not much like you — that, of course in a bathing outfit that shall be provided for you, you get into the tub and reproduce for all of us the most original deeds you performed on that illustrious January day in your garden!"

There was no escaping it. I put on the swimming trunks, climbed into the water, warm this time, thank goodness, and in the presence of both Highnesses, the princesses, princes, and highest dignitaries, to the sound of further verses of the emperor's song, I fed myself from the cauldron, at the same time chopping wood, shouting hip, hip, hooray! and shattering the bottles of alcohol and the cases of cigars . . .

However, I don't have time today to elaborate on everything that took place during the banquet; perhaps another time. —

I ended up in the emperor's bedroom. And though earlier he had been boundlessly happy, he suddenly became awfully gloomy and collapsed onto the fauteuil. Kneeling before him, I

embraced his knees. He pushed me away energetically and, seizing himself by the skull, shook his head wildly as if he wanted
to tear it from his trunk and toss it away like a worthless piece
of garbage. Next he began to wave his arms as if he were shoo-
ing mosquitoes away from his forehead. Then he jumped up,
spread his arms wide toward the east — then toward the south
— thereupon to the north and with a cry sank back onto the
fauteuil and, looking — as before — at himself continually in
the mirror, said:

"Begone, ye shadows that flit about the Kaiser's temples. Van-
ish, black cares, beneath whose burden sinks even my unbounded
strength! Oh! a heavy pall descends from every side upon the
Empire given to me by God as my fief! How I used to sense in my
prophetic ecstasies, as I now know for a fact on the basis of authoritative information, that the Chinese Boxers are contemplating
the conquest, subjugation, and destruction of My inheritance.
Daily do I discover that they are organizing and arming themselves — and against whom, if not against Me? Oh, perhaps
this very year the meads of my empire shall be inundated by the
fresh hordes of Genghis Khan — they will never forgive me for
sending Waldersee against them in my divine foreboding 12 years
ago. — And they have their allies — namely, the Boers, who are
offended that I did not grant Krüger an audience. They have
already formed an alliance for conquest and resistance against us
— and then they shall be joined by those Bohemians. And worst,
Bismarck will lead them all. Ha! loathsome traitors . . . ! The four
B's! a development omineux . . . Will my gallant people stand
firm? Ah, unbeknownst to you, Wilhelm the Great, it was not a

golden but a thorny crown that you set upon the unfortunate pate of your orphaned grandson!"

He fell silent. And I thought to myself: "From the beginning, you were always a loony crackpot of a basket case, and now it looks like you've gone clean off your rocker to boot. As for the Chinese Boxers, after all, my brother the general told me that we don't need to fear them, since they don't have any weapons; even if they were the biggest big shots in the box, how far would their fists get them in the face of our Big Berthas? The Boers, that's another cup of tea; they showed John Bull what they were made of, they're certainly our empire's most dangerous enemies. But the Bohemians? All we'd have to do is use our cannons to shoot those revolting plum dumplings of theirs at them instead of shells, they'd take to gathering them up, the voracious rabble, they'd gobble them all up, get into fistfights over them and then let themselves be easily slugged and caught like sozzled hens. And now, what about that Bismarck? Is it really possible the German Emperor doesn't know the guy has been dead for years? Or does he perhaps have an idée fixe — he was always incredibly apprehensive about him — that the old man will rise from his grave like Barbarossa from Kyffhäuser?" And unable to stand it any longer, I remarked:

"I am not certain, Majesty, but I believe Bismarck has not been among the living for some time."

He scowled severely. "Dixi!" he cried, "who dares to speak where the Imperator has expressed an opinion? Remember that everything I say is wise, merely because it is I who have said it, though coming from anyone else it would be foolish. I know what

I know. The German princes, a treacherous lot, in collusion with whom he wished to commit me to an asylum, spirited him away somewhere alive, so that at an opportune moment they and he might make their move against me. Yet quos ego!" he swore, flinging his fauteuil into the corner with some effort. "You shall be crushed like that fauteuil!" he roared on, although the armchair remained undamaged. "You shall weaken against me, you pygmies, all of you! God will continue to protect me from your wrath, God, who was my shield when the infamous Selma Schnapke flung her ax at my armor-plated carriage!"

He lifted his arms heavenward, then snorted loudly through his nose. And he continued:

"To the point! We must face the catastrophe head on, before it takes us by surprise. We have but one means at our disposal: we must found an Anti-Bebebebe-Gefahr League. I created this name myself, and immediately gave the order for the League's establishment. A great many of my vassals have donated large sums toward it. And you, dear Helmut, as always, shall be in the vanguard. You have a fortune of about 800 million marks — don't fidget, you declared only 300 million in order to cheat the state — stop shaking, I am the monarch, after all — although it is my primary obligation to see that the laws are upheld, I am willing to turn a blind eye to certain things — let us be clement toward one another, as our Father in Heaven is toward us. Well, in short, if you donate 20 million for this holy purpose, I think it would be a trifle. Consider what would become of your entire fortune if Chao-chu chiao conquered the Mark of Brandenburg at the head of his hordes! Tua res, Romane, agitur!"

"You are a swine as well!" I thought to myself. "You've already wrung 45 million out of me for — I shall not complete my thought out of regard for morality — and now another 20 million! . . . Where will all this lead me? Let those who rule bleed the workers out of house and home, that's all right, like taking milk from a cow, but us aristocrats? . . . I knew from the start what all his drivel was leading up to. That damned Hohenzollern miserliness, it's hereditary! Fritz was even worse. — Dear Fritz, with tiny Prussia you conquered Europe, but this, supposedly 'your' descendant, with an enormous Germany, would be a pushover for any who attacked *him*, even Denmark alone. Oh Fritzie, why did you bother to sire children at all? After one has scaled the heights of Mont Blanc, what else is there? After all, the descendants of great men have almost always been utter swine . . . All that came after you is just dung, dear Fritz! Bismarck, although he's not of the Hohenzollern line — merely its mystical prick — was the greatest misfortune of the German people — —."

There was nothing for me to do but say yes. "I'll make my subscription very soon, Majesty."

He made a terrible frown. "A subscription? Ugh! how like petty shopkeeping! And why not right away, dear Helmut? You always have your checks with you! Fill one out this instant — 20 million — made out to your monarch, and that shall be quite enough! Shame to the man who puts off until tomorrow . . . !"

And lightning-quick, his hand flew into my breast pocket. Everything is permitted the Imperator, even theft; that which an ordinary person calls theft is in His case only his noble Mandate, his drive to conquer, a matter of course. He fished out my wallet, a thief to the core, and as if it had always been his to run his paws through, he immediately extracted my checks and said:

"I shall bring you pen and ink, my dear Sternenhoch; the Kaiser does not deem it an indignity to serve thus one whom he calls his friend!"

Bring them he did, and I — I would have ground my teeth if I still had them — flung another 20 million into the dragon's insatiable gullet. I knew that this Bebebebe League would never see even a pfennig of it. Yet let no one think that his earlier talk was conscious artifice, a trick. That arch-liar's deception, on a gigantic scale, is ever and only for himself alone. He has no idea at all what he really thinks, what he wants; truth, falsehood, reality, illusion have all dissolved into some kind of rotting chaos, phosphorescent only in his boundless vanity . . . —

As soon as he had stuck the check in his pocket, his face suddenly brightened with incredible exultation. However, he realized this immediately; he was well disciplined in his youth; they say Bismarck thrashed him like a dog, but he evidently couldn't thrash him into any kind of respectable shape. — He frowned again. Once more he jerked his head about and drove invisible mosquitoes away from it — and then he said:

"Begone, shadows flitting about my temples! — The Kaiser has bid thee gone, and gone they are! Vicit Caesar! And he shall be victorious with the help of God, whose mills grind slowly, everywhere! Enough! And now the Kaiser wishes to be a mortal man again!"

And then his countenance quite definitely lit up. And as usual when he was in a good mood, he began to improvise in verse:*

---

* The publisher of these memoirs, unable to compose in rhyme, presents this poem in the original.

Und nun, Hellmutchen mein
lass uns recht froh und fröhlich sein!
In's weiche Bett legen wir nieder
– e – e – uns wieder
(nein, besser:)
uns're arg erschöpften Glieder.
's ist besser, in den Arsch zu ficken,
als an der Politik ersticken!
Weg Sorgen, die den Caesar drücken!
Doch halt! ich muss dir früher machen
hübsch Vergnügen – – e – e mit netten Sachen.
Ich will dir nämlich gnädig zeigen,
Fotografien, — die — mir — eigen,
im Lauf von letzten drei Monaten
jemacht – – e – e von fotografierenden — —
Ratten . . .

"Dear Helmut, have you ever seen such an improvisateur?" he then added, flushed from the effort and perhaps also with a panicked embarrassment.

But I had gone white as chalk. There would surely be at least 200 of these photographs! And do you know what that meant for me? The obligation to fall into ecstasy 200 times! I, who had just been enraged by the throwing away of 20 million! If I failed to become ecstatic even once, I would fall into disfavor. For he considered the photographs he was about to show me to be his faithful likeness and works of art from first to last, since they had been praised by Him; it was impermissible to say even: This does not compare to the original . . . If I were not to be captivated by even one of them, he would interpret that to mean: that I deplored his taste and, in addition, that I considered him a hideous creature.

Well, I fell into an unbroken chain of ecstasies for about two hours. The photographs numbered at least 500.

I had two-hundred ecstasies to go and was ready to die. But merciful nature came to the rescue. The emperor tottered on his chair such that he would have rolled onto the floor if I had not caught him. — "Ha!" he cried out, "Morpheus has embraced the Kaiser. Nothing doing, my little louse, I must deprive you of further pleasures; so much the better this way, and may there be uncommon delights reserved for you tomorrow as well . . . Well then — let's put ourselves to bed!"

I took off his Bolivian general's uniform. He nodded for me to lie down next to him — —. Fortunately, a minute later he began to snore. I looked at his open, smelly mouth, his stiff, comical features, grotesque in spite of all their grandezza . . . There was nothing more ridiculous than his face — if only it did not belong to the emperor — —

You miserable crackpot! O miserable nation! The ancient Greek military leader Chabrias said: "A herd of deer led by a lion can accomplish more than a herd of lions led by a deer." And I would say: "Would that, instead of 80 million Germans, there were only 8 million of them — and over them — a Lion, rather than — —

In some kind of dark, awful premonition I wept on that night, for You, Germania . . .

For the past fourteen days I have written nothing, not having had even a second to spare for it; I have simply been absorbed by entertainments, drinking, ladies, young men, friends, the emperor. I have been cured, absolutely! Any ballerina means more to me than — she. Hosanna!

Yet I think the suffering I had to endure practically every other day while in the monarch's presence had a greater share in my cure than all the entertainments. "Endure" — an apposite word; for although I am his most intimate acquaintance, it is almost never permitted me to sit down when with him. From the time that thief filched 20 million from my checkbook he has become more arrogant and unbearable than ever before. He no longer needs me; and, ashamed before me, he is taking revenge for my act of charity; the old adage is right when it says: "No good deed goes unpunished." But it's easy to say, don't do your monarch a good turn; he'll have your head cut off if you don't. — Every day a different torture; I sometimes envied the Daemoness her scarlet palace . . . But every cloud has its silver lining: while I was bow-ing and scraping at Willy's and kissing his boots and other things beginning with "b" — I could not spare even a thought for the Daemoness; and the rage that had long churned within me, always, even when we said adieu, amusingly dispelled all terrifying thoughts. Of course, this kind of thing is just chasing out Satan with Beelzebub; but for the moment, at least, Beelzebub isn't threatening to drive me mad. I take pride in my self-control, by which I have preserved the emperor's favor and respect undi-minished; and I shall divulge to you, O paper, that when he said goodbye to me the day before yesterday, with tears in his eyes, he told me solemnly: "I swear that the very next chancellor of the Empire shall be you, dear Helmut, you pearl of Germania!"

He has left for Spain to visit Alfonso. He won't come back for three whole weeks. — I am free of the one suffering that was left me! Now I can go carousing with Moltke and Eulenburg. Oh, the beauty of it all, to be happy again after such terrible suffering! How marvelous the world is!

April 27

Seven in the morning. My bedroom windows are open. The broad gardens spread out beneath them. Outside, all is radiance and festivity and laughter. Although it is early in both the morning and the spring — an almost summery wind comes streaming toward me from the outdoors. And the laughing sun, low until now, burns warmly. The scent of apricot and cherry blossoms wafts toward me like the mystical greetings of enchanting wind-spirits. The lake of trees below me cries noisily with the bright songs of innumerable little birds. The clouds in the sky smile down upon me — how gladly I would fly up to you, my silver-golden doves, and travel through the timeless, blue wilderness on your little backs! . . . I can't sit at home any longer — oh, to soar with Eulenburg and Moltke up into nature! —

The same day, 11 at night in a wine bar

It was a marvelous day. We left Berlin, the three of us, by automobile, but along the way we picked up some splendid ladies and dashing waiters . . . Oh, what a beautiful time we all had in the forests and restaurants, the meadows, invisible hollows, and brothels! It was the most splendid day of my life! . . . While driving into Berlin, intoxicated by everything possible, I suddenly had a rather awful feeling: I had reached my peak! . . .

I entered my apartment by myself and stopped at the threshold terribly frightened: red beams lit the room so hellishly that I could see only blood, blood . . . In spite of the temptation to turn back, I went forward; ohh, why did I ever do so! . . . It seemed to me that I could smell a corpse. My heart leapt into my throat, and without knowing why, I was running around like a scared rabbit, when I saw — Her. On top of a tall cabinet, just below the ceiling, she was sitting and swinging her legs, which were hanging down. Her gaze was sly, mocking, venomous. In her hand she held a rope tied into a noose, and she was swinging it over her head . . . At that moment I still had the strength to dash out into the corridor; yet once there I sank to my knees. —

April 30

So now, lucky me, I'm back where I was before the first of April, when I left for Berlin; and all of a sudden. Moreover, I have been cast much further backward than before. Not only have I been revisited by the full force of that terrible pain over the eternal damnation of my wife, and not only do I have a fresh, new fear — of her noose —: but I have conceived a deep horror of her ghost more powerful than any I have ever known before. None of her previous appearances was as frightening for me as this last one. All my wounds, which were nearly closed, have again been opened wide; I have had not a moment's rest; I have lost all my appetite for pleasure; every attempt to get a hold of myself has been useless . . . The only thing that helps a little is getting drunk out of my gourd; but this inevitably leads to the indirect acceleration — — of the terrible end . . .

Yet what I am most frightened by is the awful fact that many concepts have become terribly confused for me, more so than usual. Things have changed beyond compare since January. Then, my incipient ravings were the result of horrible, long-term disturbances and a lengthy series of visions; yet this time a single hallucination has done the trick, even after a sustained period of rest and manifest improvement in my health — and I'm in it deeper than before. It has already become stuck in my shattered organism. I am falling into an abyss, slowly, but surely. My God, is there no help for me? . . .

Of course, I still have the Podex romanus; but it does not have absolute power; it must be accompanied by those magic words. Could I possibly have invoked them in time on that fateful evening? It is time for a thoroughgoing reform. Ever since that rencontre in the park I have been resolved that, for as long as I live, I shall not take a book into my hand; I wish that keeping all my resolutions presented as little difficulty as the keeping of this one. But avoiding books — that's not enough. I must e.g., always shout out my incantation before I open a door; or before I look back over my shoulder; or whenever a lady with a figure similar to that of the Daemoness and wearing a veil comes in my direction. In general, I must have those words constantly on my lips, no less often than the word "I." Today I made a beginning: three ladies wearing veils were coming in my direction; I yelled, turning my backside toward them and bending forward of course: "Up my ass, etc." They had my papers checked by a policeman. But even so, it's certainly better than the Daemoness.

Yet these new measures have considerably calmed me; I look to the future with full confidence.

May 4

Dear folk, for the sake of the Lord Christ, I tell you, I spoke with her again! In the forest, can you believe it? Next to me there was a tree. And just think, today she even came driving up! In a carriage! And dressed in men's clothes! And a whip in her hands! But she didn't thrash me. And if you had heard the way she spoke! Well, I'll tell you all about it, only I must be careful not to — not to jump over the box of matches there, or better said, not to get my ideas mixed up. You know, it seems to me that I'm going a little crazy. But that will pass, won't it? Everything passes; even a goat's got to kick the bucket sometime. And just so you know, she would not have come if I had shouted you-know-what in time. But if you had seen her in those men's clothes! A short coat, tight-fitting, thin green trousers, hot damn, you should have seen that tummy of hers and her rear end under them! — Well, then:*

So, yesterday I left with Moltke Jr. and Eulenburg for Berlin again. At 11 in the morning we stopped at a restaurant in the forest, just 200 paces from its edge. I had been sitting with them for just a little while when I felt such a great and awkward sense of restlessness that I got up to take a little walk.

---

* We have deleted from the following passage the lunatic ravings with which it is saturated.

I walked out of the forest. Close to its edge ran the highway. A sunny, warm, exquisite day. My soul was sweetly soothed by the mildly hilly countryside with its small cottages dispersed across the low slopes like little sheep; it was soothed until it was hypnotized . . . I went traipsing along the highway.

Suddenly I gave a start, like a person dozing off; I heard the rumble of wheels, the stamping of hooves. A two-wheeled carriage came rushing toward me. Two soot-black horses in front of it. It was bearing down on me as fast, no exaggeration, as an express train. "Runaway horses!" I took fright and leaped into the forest. It was high time I did: that get-up from hell was right on top of me. It stopped almost instantly, and a man with a riding crop in his hand jumped out — and came directly toward me. I looked sharp — the Daemoness. Once again I sat down; this time in a patch of bramble, but I didn't feel its thorns.

Her face — hellfire transformed into human flesh. Never before had I seen her so wild, terrible — and so triumphant. If the faces of all the Caesars and Napoleons were to merge harmoniously into one, they would not emit half of the transcendent commanderliness that sparkled from her in a thousand flashes. And she looked as young again as a girl, a rosy flush on her white face: a fire blazing triumphantly in the snow! An alto, superterrestrial voice boomed — the peal of a Roman cymbal, of the archangels' trumpets, summoning to the Last Judgment:

"Since that day when you were sitting in the mud, much has changed. I now look upon my situation differently, ha ha! I no longer regard you as a phantom in my dream. You are indeed my husband, that old dog. And I categorically demand an explanation of what took place on the nineteenth of August!"

"I — I — don't know anything. Ask a doctor — science . . . I had nothing to do with it, I'm just a phantom in your dream —"

"Any old scoundrel could easily say that he is a mere phantom in order to escape punishment. Listen, you lowlife: I have grasped that the nineteenth of August was not as decisive for me as the second of September, when I left the vault . . . More precisely: that I did not dream the vault, that it was 'reality,' that I — — died in a dungeon . . ."

"Ai, ai! . . . But I'm surprised that you, a woman at least somewhat schooled in science, are talking like this. How in the world could you have died if you are here and speaking? How could you even exist or think if your brain is now rotting?"

"The hell with science, you moron! It's even more moronic than you. *Your* brain is rotting, and you can still think, although rottenly. All the brains of all the people in the world are rotting and *all* the thoughts of human culture are *only* the products of the most putrid rottenness: I bring this great truth from beyond the grave! To the point! I was hit in the head by someone and then cast into the dungeon. Who was it?"

"Oh God — you don't really think that — I?" came stupidly out of me.

"You?" she guffawed. "You old woman, you capable of such a thing? Unthinkable. But it is not unthinkable that you cravenly arranged for someone to carry it out. Yet it is more probable that it was done by one of your cretinous relatives unhappy with my lifestyle. Perhaps with your agreement; apparently with your knowledge; yet quite certainly you did nothing to prevent it. Well —?"

She raised her riding crop. Her face — a fusion of tiger and Lucifer. "She's been promoted in hell" — the thought flashed through my mind, "from a tortured, damned soul to one of the devils who does the torturing." Every fiber of my brain went buzzing like a taut string, and the cottages on the slopes were jumping all over the place like they were drunk and embracing the fences of their yards, dancing madly. I had the distinct sensation that I was standing on my head.

"I am innocent — I'm a phantom — I'm a phantom —"

"If you're a phantom, it won't matter to you if I thrash you!"

"No, no — oh, Jesus and Mary! I'm not a phantom, please, please! What I told you in the park was the truth. You disappeared from the castle so suddenly, before I arrived with the doctor, and you were sleeping in the forest. There is no doubt on that score, look into it yourself. But I shall give the order right away for that accursed forest to be searched, I myself will search it, Willy will help me, and we'll wake you up —"

Suddenly she burst out laughing: "Wake me up — what for? to this scabious dream of yours? Mine is altogether better!"

All at once she was laughing so gaily. You don't know how gratifying this was, coming after her earlier fury. Roused with courage, I said to her:

"Oh, wife of mine, how marvelous you look today! Like a rosebud, like a Madonna! And plump as a bun! What a tummy you have! You're doing well there, aren't you? What do they cook up for you there?"

I was frightened by my bravery. Yet at that moment she — would you believe it? stroked my face very tenderly, but immediately afterward gave me a slap — a very small one; then she wiped her hand on her pants and collapsed on the ground, right in front of me. She wept convulsively, shuddered feverishly, and suddenly embraced my knees. But right away she fell back onto her face: — What was going on inside of her? . . .

And just at that moment, the noon hour chimed from the hillside, so tenderly childlike. She rose unexpectedly and — can you believe it? snatched the handkerchief into which I myself had just been weeping and dried her eyes with it. Yet she then immediately threw it away. She sat down near me and spoke, violently at first; from her bitten-through lip welled drops of blood.

"I'm feeling talkative — I'll tell you, Prince, what has happened to me since March. Oh! Oh! . . . What beauty!" Her eyes shone . . . And at that point she joyously lit up a Virginia cigar — and took a swig from a bottle containing a white liquid. She gave a shudder and her eyes teared up. And I smelled the sharp tang of 192-proof liquor . . . During her lifetime, you see, she drank undiluted spirits — and not even after death did she neglect this vice! What a routine! What a routine!

"Well, that day we talked in the gardens was a big turning point in my fate. As the hurricane was taking hold of me, I recalled that in my sufferings I *must* summon my *Will*, all-overcoming, Absolute, perceiving all beneath Itself; I also recalled some of the unpleasant practices, obvious in waking, unknown in dreams, involved in its summoning. Despite all my dark, mad striving, I had no success in the first torture chambers. Ten rooms I went through. My suffering in the eleventh was more terrible than ever before. But pain intensifies spiritual activity beyond measure. It strained, in connection with the most terrible, violent striving, my entire soul to such an inexpressible, mystical degree that a miracle took place: a flame flared up from the middle of the water! *in my dream* a luminous, self-assured, *awakening* Will shone forth! one that was self-embracing, all-shattering, all-creating, all-powerful, all-knowing — the core of Being itself. And from its self-embrace I quickly extracted ideas: everything, even that which is most terrible, is merely plasma, the absolute game of My Will, here only so that it might find affirmation of that fact in its own supreme, untarnished delight, as it sovereignly, violently plays with everything, eternally winning for winning's sake alone; only to the extent that this is misunderstood does menace exist for the soul, does suffering, does Evil exist; in the instant of that comprehension everything is changed into pure Radiance — a supersolar, uniform Radiance; all particulars, parts, differences disappear, all is transformed into One, eternally unchanging, immutable and absolute; all pains are only false inferences based on the error that anything can cause harm; know that in Eternity everything brings only benefit, and every suffering will suddenly melt into a white delight, into My Gloriole eternal, which is light and light alone, which is I, myself . . . This knowledge par excellence blazed boundlessly bright, accompanied by the thunderous clamor of Superbliss — — suddenly, even my most intense bodily pains changed into the most intense spiritual and bodily delight, such as I had never felt before. All, all was now

Super-radiance, Supermusic. The north pole had suddenly become the equator. 'The indescribable — has here become reality!'

"In the outgoing tide of that Divine state I became aware that the enormous building was swaying as if there were an earthquake, that the droning of the machines and the cries of the condemned had stilled — that the torturing monsters were shrieking in desperation — that one of them had seized me and thrown me out the window . . .

"My consciousness disappeared. On regaining it, I was different than in my previous, bearable dreams: I had Will . . . and as a result my dreaming was now actually 'waking,' — without the limitations of waking, it was a higher synthesis of waking and dreaming. I was now able to think distinctly — if it seemed to you when you were in the mud that day that I was thinking clearly, you were only projecting the distinctness of your waking state into my chaos. I began to recall the many, many things that had been shrouded in veils for me. The main thing is, I understood that I was 'dead.' That is something none of the dead wants to understand; the idea 'I have expired' is lethal to one who has thus far been rooted in this 'life' of yours. At first I was taken aback by this idea as well; but a moment later I was laughing at my idiotic mistake: for the whole of your waking is but a terrible error, born of Omni-idiocy. One must be God; everything else having to do with humanity is dung. —

"The next hurricane didn't come, though I passionately wished for it. It wasn't going to come later, either. The devils in the scarlet palace did not want me any longer; they saw me as a lice-infested sheep whom it was necessary to expel from the institute. But God — which is my Self — has ordained otherwise.

"One time that cur — the hurricane — came at me again unexpectedly. I screamed all the way through three rooms, but in the fourth one the same thing happened, though more intensely, as before in the eleventh one. They threw me out again, in a hurry; the walls of the palace were cracking . . .

"And I went there two times more. Just pro forma. The monsters bestowed torments upon me that were deliberately quite bearable. It was no worse than being beaten. And at the same time I had the feeling we usually have when we dream we are being beaten: it is far more pleasant than painful; every dream is masochistic; masochism is a basic fact. — I enjoyed hell. Now I am almost sorry that I have decided I shall destroy them.

"I have not yet reached the final, greatest Victory. Otherwise I would not still be constantly sent into hell. My work is not yet done. My Eternal Providence evidently wants me to scatter them once and for all, to transform them into an Elysian Inferno; the battle that shall decide my fate still awaits me — ah, Great Divine Decision!

"But how am I to wage this fateful battle when the devil's troops flee before me from afar? Yet it must come about. Who will win? . . . I see clearly the enemy's position and the state of my forces:

"They will inject a substance into me: the substance of divine beings in the non-spatial reaches of the All-ness, shining over all the suns yet eternally inert, without parallax. These substances render the human soul capable of enduring many hours of pain whose hundredth part would otherwise, like lightning, kill anyone. Also another substance from the gods that evokes a purely mental suffering — the most horrible, monstrous, metaphysical ideas, against which the most terrible that the Dream of man can offer is like a molehill compared to the mountains on the moon. And a third substance that causes all the nerves to become a hundred times more sensitive than before, and all of them suddenly to feel the absolute maximum somatic and psychological pain; compared to this *all-out* torture, all the agonies known to you humans are a moronic joke.

"This will surely last only a moment more, which will, however, be like an eternity. Even without the onrush of Will, Pain will surely turn automatically into delight. For I have obtained, in spite of the laws of the Dream, Will — suffering thus falls on barren soil: Pain is nothing other than a surrogate for an inadequate Will. All the waves of torment are deflected from that rock where they expected to find loose topsoil instead. Here, decision is already victory. My victory is assured beforehand; it shall be but a meager harvest that follows the monstrous sowing of previous victories. — And I merely observe: the gods use this suffering, which awaits me still, only as a raffinement of Their Delight, as a stimulant to Bliss Eternal; suffering for them is just delight to the second power. —

"And that second of time shall sweep away the scarlet palace, and all those that are like it in the all-ness, more effectively than a million tons of ecrasite. I shall redeem endless legions of souls by my suffering. That which Christ did not manage to accomplish: to overcome hell, I will . . .

"Yet — the all-saving hurricane is not coming. I have no opportunity . . . Alas, if I don't manage to create it myself! . . .

"What am I doing nowadays? I live the life of a goddess! I fly through the universe a thousand times faster than light and experience endless pleasures, immersing myself in its curious, ever-so-comic depths. My soul shines more intensely than the souls of all the people that have ever existed; and where it shines, all fall adoringly at its feet! I am the queen of the universe. Oh! only when Woman awakens from the sleep in which she has been sub-merged since the age of the spiders . . . , only when she tramples out that vulgar, idiotic, degenerate, parasitic, most ridiculous breed of males, will its sun shine on humanity! — I fly through the non-spatiality of ideas rather than through space. I have definitively solved a global problem; wiped out skepticism; all my nights have been transformed into endless suns. I recall the whole of eternity behind me. Except for that one silly thing, who that noble character was, that and that alone!" She chortled. "But most of all I keep to the Cordilleras, in a palace carved out of ice, with a view of the Ocean and of — His eyes . . . Oh! although we have died, we have found each other! But He is cross with me . . . In all my glory I do not impress Him in the least. He always wants from me, always wants the same old thing from me . . . , other-wise He says I will fall again . . . —"

She covered her face with her palms; and a moment later she spoke, in a whisper, in an altered voice:

"There is one thing I am afraid of . . . Of a kind of black hole that is more horrible than everything I have overcome . . . And that black hole — is me, me through and through . . . And then that white, slug-like ghost. For me that is blacker still. Ah, ah, I am nothing but black, eternal hatred. This isn't the way I'll become victorious . . . I love; but my love is only a small island in the sea of my hatred. I have a will; but she is a ruler in exile, a slave to black lands. I am black. That is why my ghost is white; that is why light is for me — a ghost . . . My Man is right, this isn't the way I'll become victorious . . ."

She collapsed again; suddenly she bounced up and, Lord God in the heavens, she gave me a little kiss . . . And she fell back on her face and writhed on the ground. At that moment she bounced up like a ball and yelled:

"Love is a swinish weakling, hatred is all! Unworthy of hatred, as a certain celebrated cur has said, is Self! only everything that is not Self, in fact, what by a stupid error does not appear to be it! The error of Omni-idiocy is worthy of hatred! The error that something exists outside of me! That's the whole wretched universe. It should be smashed. Man of mine, as dead as I, you are a moral wretch like all men! I shall win my struggle without you, I spit on you! Only Woman is Man! — — Enough of ignoble talk with you, you rat from the cloaca! You have been initiated into death, the most terrible thing of all. You chancre, believe me: you have only the fact that you treat my kittycats tolerably well at Saustein to thank that you are still stinking in the light of your fecal sun! But once I find out what part you had in that dungeon of your degenerate ancestors, believe you me, I'll cast you into the most horrible of hells, I the Queen of Hells, I the Queen of the Heavens, I Eternity's Queen!"

Having given me a kick, she drank some more, like a cow. "Helga," I muttered, half-dead, "don't drink those spirits! I tell you, they'll destroy you."

She chuckled. "Do you know what nectar the gods drink? Pure spirits! Take a swig yourself!" And she thrust the bottle into my mouth.

I took a sip. "More, you beast! — More! Or I'll wallop you! — That's right, then, so you'll have something to remember me by!" . . .

She ran to the coach, but she was staggering noticeably. She clambered onto the driver's box with difficulty, and those black stallions, surely devils in her service, broke into a mad gallop. In a moment their stamping and the clatter of the wheels subsided — —

Suddenly, half-conscious, I gave a start — something was attacking me, I felt blows on my shoulder. I shifted my eyes — Prince Eulenburg and Moltke! "By jiminy!" cried the latter, "what are you doing sitting here so abjectly, my little brother so sweet? And in the brambles, praise the Lord's every spirit!" They picked me up. "Oh," moaned Moltke, "your sweet little heinie certainly has been pricked! — really, there's blood on your trousers! Oh Willy, Willy, you would shed tears of blood if you could see this."

Enough! The reader has already seen that I am a lunatic; what else could have become of me after this terrible episode? She even drove up today in a coach, halt! she was smoking a Virginia cigar and drinking spirits, what a bitter pill! Good Christians, what have things come to when someone rotting half a year in a dungeon goes around guzzling spirits like a cow at the same time? O tempora, o mores! And she was wearing men's clothes, the vagrant! You should have seen that tummy of hers, those cheeks of her behind! That time in the park she looked like a cat who'd given birth to kittens. Oh, you tummy that I once caressed on my wedding night, if I had known then under what circumstances I would lay eyes on you again — — —

It is now midnight. It's a miracle that I have written all this down, today of all days. But it was her liquor that caused this and nothing else. It got me high as a kite, and that saved me from going absolutely crazy. Would you believe it, my throat was still burning, even hours later? Moltke and Eulenburg could smell it on me, and though they searched my pockets and the surrounding area for a bottle, they found nothing. They shook their heads; of course, I didn't tell them how it happened . . . Even if I had wanted to, my burning tongue, stiff as a board, could not have.

May 6

I am constantly three sheets to the wind. Drunkenness is madness; I am proceeding homeopathically, banishing the devil with Beelzebub. And look how exquisitely it works. Now I really am a lunatic, but since I'm always soused . . . no one takes any notice; if it weren't for the fact that I'd spent the last few days drunk without letup, with faithful friends looking after me, I'd be sitting in the loony bin now. But what's more: I'd *really* be mad. A great many of the most reasonable people end up in the loony bin, and almost everyone walking freely on the street belongs in a loony bin.

Now I'm drunk all over again. Where am I? . . . Oh, yes — still in Berlin. Willy is in the Balearic Islands, with Alfonso . . . But you, Daemoness, you filthy swine, don't toy with me! I'm warning you! If you appear before me one more time, I'll have you picked up by the police, I, your husband . . . The cuckold. You'll pay with your own blood for — — killing me . . . It makes me weep. And I have — always — loved you, more with each passing day . . .

That stuff you were babbling about the destruction of hell is flat-out nonsense. Hell is a work of God, it is a House, a Divine Cathedral, kapeesh? If the Lord God could see it now —. You adulterous bitch — you grew proud in your conceit when you were promoted to the rank of devil, like a hireling who has become the boss over his old buddies, or even a member of parliament. But I'll give you what for! Of course, you're a devil now, you have the power to carry me off to hell any time, oh Lord —

But the main thing is: wasn't that bitch — alive after all? Where did she get those horses? and those green trousers? Would a ghost have lost its footing like she did when climbing onto the coach? And those spirits of hers, hoo boy, it must have been the real thing if I had to keep clearing my throat afterward all the way until evening . . .

She was lying in the tower, pink and white, like a pig in a butcher shop. These problems would be enough to drive me loony, if I weren't already a lunatic.

The reason for this entire unfortunate affair is that she was wearing men's clothes, and it didn't occur to me to yell out in time — you know what. It is time for reform. Starting today, I will scream my catchphrase at everyone I meet, woman or man. Hallelujah! Therein lies my salvation. I've calmed down. Everything's going to be all right.

I am at Saustein. For this reason: in Berlin I simply cannot permit myself the freedom to shout my spell so incessantly. I shouted it in front of an officer who had a stature like hers . . . He gave me such a slap that I'm still seeing sparks before my eyes today. He shall be suspended, I have already given the order; though the slap remains. But at Saustein, everyone far and wide knows me, and here they will accept my slogan with all due reverence.

As I was shouting it today along the edges of my property, all the village men and women bent down to the ground.

As the English say: All right! All I have to do is drink a lot and I'm saved. But — may God protect me from another one of her appearances. I feel this absolutely: if this should happen, I'm done for.

Hee hee hee hee! Esteemed public! Prince Sternenhoch is honored to announce to the Dearly Beloved that yesterday and today the following events of great importance took place: first of all, the Daemoness whipped me like a horse. Secondly, I spent the night in the stable on top of a baby calf which had a black snout and in the rear, a tail. Thirdly, the spirit of my deceased St. Bernard, Elephant, entered into me. Fourthly, I opened the Podex romanus. Fifthly, I visited Esmeralda Carmen Kuhmist and received her blessing. Sixthly, I tussled with some policemen, in return for which they thrashed me at the police station until I stank. Seventhly, whoever wishes to find me now must come to the madhouse.

But let no one presume me mad. Yesterday I was, a little, although now, at this moment, I am entirely in possession of my faculties; this is evidently the result of that most regrettable drubbing at the police station. And also of the knowledge that I would get rays from the planet Aldebaran from old lady Kuhmist. I shall now proceed to tell the story without fine phrases and ornamentation, draping no empty frippery and finery onto the narrative thread, hey ho! huzzah!

So then, yesterday evening I was sitting in my bedroom at Saustein. Being somewhat drunk, I was drowsing. Then I heard a rustling in the next room — and then such soft footfalls, as if a tiger were walking there, tyap, tyap, tyap . . . The door was locked, of course, and even the keyhole was stopped up with wax. After that, some hands began to rub against the door from top to bottom and from bottom to top . . . But I was already well aware of what was going on! Jump up my ass! I roared and kept roaring like a lion until the chateau shook. Naturally, I was bent over with my backside facing the door as I shouted . . . And then between my legs, behind me, I suddenly caught sight of — ladies' shoes! And they were walking! I straightened up and beheld Her . . .

I did not fall down but ran out into the corridor. However, she was right behind me — stomp! stomp! stomp! "I'll teach you some manners, you ignorant stable boy!" she screamed and whipped me like a horse. All the way through the corridor and down the stairs to the ground floor.

I saved myself in the servants' quarters; the servants armed themselves with long-handled brushes and pokers and grr! went out to get her. But they found nothing. I had a mind to spend the night in the servants' quarters; but I felt like I was going to start babbling some awful nonsense. I went off to the stable and lay down in the dampness, next to the abovementioned baby calf that had a black snout and in the rear, a tail. It harbored no unfriendly intentions toward me; and it was certainly not afraid of the Daemoness either; nor was I. I am never afraid of her in the stable; if she came there, I would kick her like a horse . . .

I did not sleep. I was thinking about my St. Bernards, who were with the Lord. Hot damn, if they'd been with me when she started to whip me, what would have been left of her! . . . And I had them executed . . . To no end and for no reason, in fact. What a clod I am! . . . I was weeping for them until right then I felt: they haven't died, they've become incarnate in me, particularly Elephant. His strength surged all through my limbs, and I started to run around on all fours and bark and bite the cows on their thighs — —

But above all, anger toward Kuhmist was boiling within me. "Nasty witch," I yelled, "not even that catchphrase helps any more, even against punches to the head. And the Podex romanus stopped working even before that! I'll take a look inside, now that it's lost its power, at least let me see what the rays of Aldebaran, the droppings of a viper, a frog's quill, and gorilla tears look like!"

I tore the thread — and do you know, ladies and gentlemen, what was inside the nut? Nothing, honest-to-goodness nothing at all! "Treacherous swine!" I bellowed, "you'll pay for this with your life! First thing tomorrow I'm going to the emperor, and he'll have you burned alive, quartered, hung!"

When the day began to dawn, I ran out of the stable, raced

into my rooms, and took my calling card and two bundles of 1000-mark banknotes, with a 100-count in each; and I flew hot-footed to the train station. I left on the same clothes I had been wearing when lying next to the baby calf. And this was wise of me. For the people at the train station and in the train took me for a drunken stable boy, otherwise they would certainly have said I was a madman. As far as I remember, during the train ride I was barking at the passengers and snapping at their calves; but everyone just laughed at that.

On reaching Berlin, I stormed into Kuhmist's apartment like an angel of vengeance.

"You viper! You viper!" I cried, thrusting the nut up her nose. "It was empty, you she-devil, empty, arf, arf, arf!" — She became frightened, but immediately regained her composure. "Sir, conduct yourself rationally, or I shall be forced to call for help!"

"The Podex romanus — empty! arf! arf!" And getting down on all fours, I snapped at her calves; she ran away, and for some time I chased her up and down the length of the room. "I'll have you executed, by the emperor! He'll have to quarter you with his own hands! Do you know whom you have swindled? Prince Helmut Sternenhoch, the emperor's foremost favorite and advisor, and the greatest pillar of the German Empire, arf! arf! arf!"

"That's nice," she said, waving a broom in front of my head, "only begging your pardon, you look more like His Excellency's stable boy. If you please, you smell like a barn and like — moonshine —."

"Well then, here you have my identification!" and I threw my calling card at her.

"That's nice, but it is possible that the gentlemanly prince lost it somewhere — or that you —"

"I will identify myself to you more precisely!" And taking out the two wads of bills, I tore off their bands and threw it all in the air.

The black priestess paled. Several times she looked back and forth at the banknotes and at me — and then sank to her knees before me — —:

"Oh, Your Excellency, your kind forgiveness! for not recognizing you immediately on seeing your sovereign face and all your majestic appearance! Oh, what happiness to see you under my very own roof!"

"Explain yourself, an empty Podex romanus! Arf! arf! I am Elephant, Elephant!"

"Your Excellency, kindly forgive me, but you bear some of the responsibility yourself. You were not pleased to give me your address, otherwise I would have informed you of the catastrophe that has recently taken place. Ah, ah . . . An eclipse of the planet Aldebaran has occurred, inasmuch as the moon hath come between it and the sun; and for this reason the powerful Aldebaran, weeping bitterly, has ordered that all his rays, wandering throughout the world, return to him immediately, to give him new light. And thus it happened that even the rays imprisoned within the Podex romanus, flying headlong out of it, decamped to the planet Aldebaran."

"That is all true, but there were also droppings, tears, and a frog quill there!"

"Yes, Excellency, but as the rays of Aldebaran absorbed all of this into themselves, these substances likewise vanished from the nut. Everything fades, Excellency, nothing lasts forever; would you like the substances implanted inside the nut to be an exception?"

I had to admit she was right; her deep knowledge of nature was impressive. I said, more temperately:

"Arf! arf, And what next? Yesterday that maltster whipped me like a horse!"

"Have no fear, Excellency. All that is needed is to capture new rays from Aldebaran, which will shine again with undiminished brightness. For I already possess the remaining substances."

"And when can you catch them for me?"

"In a week at most, Excellency. But" — she suddenly broke down in tears — "my glass trap has broken — and it is expensive — I am a poor, wretched woman, oy, oy!"

"What does it cost?"

"I'm afraid to say. 2000 marks . . ."

"Here, take four."

"Oh, Your Eminence!" she kissed my feet. But a moment later she broke out in tears afresh. "I forgot, oh ach, that my gorilla tears have dried up. But fortunately there is a specimen of this rare ape in the zoological garden. She has just had young. If we were to purloin the infant from her, she would weep and wail and shed bitter tears, yet — as luck would have it! Her keeper loves her like his own child and would not cause her grief for anything in the world . . . For anything in the world — unless he received good compensation to do so . . ."

"Very much?"

"My God! at least — 5000 marks!"

"What idiocy, take ten thousand!"

"Oh, Your Highness, now you are saved! However — oh, Omnipotent One — it cannot be, it cannot . . . Oh, forgive me — and take your money back!"

"What — what — arf! Sweet Jesus and Mary —." I began to weep.

"Your Highness, I promised God I would never engage in magic again. Just think, the salvation of my soul is at stake . . . —"

"Christ the Lord, this can't be! Just once, I beg you, God will forgive you, the salvation of *my* soul is at stake . . . —"

"Ah, ah . . . However, I remember now: today the Virgin Mary appeared to me in a dream and said: 'On his way to see you, dear Kuhmist, is Prince Sternenhoch, the most noble, the most generous aristocrat in the world, with a plea that you give him a Podex romanus. And I permit you to do so with the condition that you have 1000 masses performed for the souls in purgatory.' Yet each one costs 20 marks, Grace, oh, I am an impoverished woman . . ."

"That's all? Arf, arf! This is 20,000 — here you go — and why don't you take all of what's left, there's 200,000, Prince Sternenhoch is no skinflint, arf, arf!"

"Oh, Your Majesty —" I shall not describe how she acted. But all of a sudden she seized me: "Now I respectfully ask that His Majesty leave me, for my thoughts on the problem of catching the rays of Aldebaran are already working intensively, and I have not a moment to waste." And she pushed me outside.

"Why are you calling me Majesty? I'm not an emperor, I am Elephant, arf, arf!"

"But you will become emperor!" she exclaimed rapturously. "My prophetic vision has read this in your venerable face. In a short time the emperor will make you his chancellor, yet you shall so excel in your high renown that our monarch will deem you worthy of his throne, and on descending from it, will seat you upon it. However, let us not waste time, Majesty, leave your servant now, having first accepted my blessing, that the powers of hell not harm you before that time when the Podex romanus again comes to rest on your heart!"

She spat on her palm and rubbed the spit around, while I howled for joy. Then, rubbing my forehead, she spoke the mysterious words:

"Hocus pocus kootch-kootchy-koo, alacazam and bobbity-boo!"

And hardly had she finished when a divine spirit entered into my body. I embraced, yelping, the precious woman, but she, bowing humbly, quickly shoved me out the door. —

A stupendous happiness drove my steps on the street so that I was nearly running. I felt like letting off some steam by yelling, jumping, barking, but I restrained myself. Then I saw a booze joint. I had never been in such a dive; yet I had a longing for something wet just now. I went in and ordered myself a rye whiskey. Then I looked for my money. Nothing anywhere, not even a pfennig . . . "So how about it, mister?" the owner of the joint came down on me, when my rummaging failed to yield anything.

"Hold your horses, you huckster," I said, "you won't lose your money on me, I being Prince Sternenhoch."

"You, Prince Sternenhoch, you dungpit?" he guffawed. "Well, pay up then, pay up, or I'll get the police, you scoundrel!"

All my noble blood was boiling. "You knave," I cried, "pay *you?* Well, that takes the cake!"

"You're coming with me to the police!"

He dragged me toward the door. But I didn't give up just like that. He pulled at me for a while and then said: "You wouldn't be worth it, you bum, for me to dirty myself with you!" And opening the door and kicking me in the rear end, he put me out on the street.

Believe me, I didn't feel the least sense of shame, on the contrary, a triumphant satisfaction that I had avoided payment. That, like the alcohol seeping into my brain, heightened my exhilaration. Suddenly I took to running, shouting: "Hey, hey, Aldebaran, planet of red! Gorilla tears, arf, arf! I am Elephant and the German Emperor! Move aside, you vermin, the emperor is passing!"

At first the passersby laughed, and then they started running with me, all the way around me. The street was chortling and kicking up a ruckus. At this moment someone yanked me backward.

A cop. "What's all the racket for, buddy?"

"What, you slave?" I roared and gave him a good, square punch.

He took hold of me and dragged me to the police station. Yet I, barking victoriously, put up a glorious fight. Only when two others had arrived did they overpower me. But hurling myself to the ground, I thrashed all about, kicking and biting. They caught me by the arms and legs and carried me away. "This guy is probably insane," one gentleman told them; "be careful with the wretch!" "Him, insane? He's drunk as a pig, get a whiff of the cheap booze on him!"

"I am not drunk, I am Prince Sternenhoch become Elephant! Let me go, you knaves, or the wrath of the emperor shall fall terribly on your heads!"

But everyone around me only laughed. And I was already at the police station. Before I could say "jew," they threw me on a bench, tied me to it, pulled off my trousers, and having taken off their belts, all of them went after me at the same time . . . Ow, ow!

Then the police commissioner came in. "Look, chief, sir, this muckheap says he's Prince Sternenhoch!" The commissioner, also taking off his belt, stood over me — — — "Sweet Jesus and Mary — stop right now, it's His Excellency — the first magnate of the empire — the chief advisor and favorite of the emperor — heaven help us — ceiling, ceiling, fall on me! — we're doomed — —"

What followed, I do not know, having fainted. Only toward evening did I regain consciousness. I am lying in a beautiful room; but one can see right away that it is not an ordinary room like people live in. My thoughts are completely muddled. But my lunacy has evidently subsided. Several people are waiting on me respectfully. I feel ill, so ill . . . It has been an act of sheer heroism that I wrote so much of this on the very same evening. But now I can no longer — I am falling asleep — — —

May 12, afternoon

I slept long; but I had awfully wild dreams. Now I am only a bit loony; at the same time, I am raving in a fever. And this is, I think, well and good. After all, delirium is nothing other than madness, bona fide madness. Madness gets lost in raving. And perhaps disappears within it . . . I recall with horror the muddle of my thinking yesterday. God, You are near me after all! Even that beating yesterday probably did me some good. At least while I was getting it, my dementia disappeared completely.

But physically I'm doing terribly. I feel so unwell, so weak, I'm shaking with cold, and my head hurts terribly. I feel deathly ill. Yet even this shall perhaps be for the best. Back in January it was illness that saved me. Of course, my madness then was not as great as it is now; and my illness not as serious as the one whose maw now awaits me . . .

Oh, God, whatever will become of me? But since I've made it this far, things will turn out, somehow —.

May 13, late evening

The clock keeps tick-tocking, it's really enough to drive a person up the wall; what stupid clod invented this pussyfooted ghost? My guards are snoring away in the room next door. And the electric light is also a capital kind of ghost. I am sitting awake in bed, but I wouldn't be able to get up from it if I tried; some scoundrel has poured mercury into my legs and into all my veins. I'm raving a little, but things could be worse right now. After all, I'm writing very rationally. What to write about? I would most like to write about the baby calf that is not afraid of the Daemoness, having a black nose; but this would not be quite worthy of the future German Emperor. Do you think I'm going crazy? Prr! I'll slip out of madness like a mouse from a pair of trousers, you'll see!

I'll write about what I heard this evening. Four people visited me: my uncle, my brother, one fat and one thin person. These people were presented to me as Bavarian noblemen; but because they spoke as if they were well-read, I recognized right away that they were no noblemen.

My uncle is an imposing figure. On the one hand, he has almost no forehead, and if one wants to make out his little eyes one must use a magnifying glass; at the same time, however, he has a formidable jaw and cheeks and a frightful moustache. Inasmuch as he is also large and robust, he evokes everywhere the utmost respect. And it increases if one hears that powerful, crackly, sluggish voice of his; the way in which Uncle speaks will be seen at once.

At the same time, my brother is merely the degenerate descendant of his illustrious forebears. He's like a cobweb, always fidgeting like a sparrow, and if you so much as breathed on him you would blow him away. He is always prattling nonsense, being a little weak in the head, and he has various speech defects. Nor is there in him even the first sign of character. The emperor values him excessively, however, and has made him a general. —

After they had spoken with me, they went into the neighboring room and discussed me. Quietly, but I understood every word; to this day I have ears like a jackass.

"Gentlemen," said the thin one, "His Excellency's disease is puzzling, heretofore unknown; but my keen eye has ascertained its cause, and psychopathology will henceforth be enriched by one additional syndrome, which I shall immediately christen: Morbus sedatorius doctoris Trottelhund. — The unfortunate patient suffers from sitting disease: he is constantly, irresistibly compelled to sit down, wherever he may be standing, and he would even sit down on red-hot coals, as he sat down on the pavement with the policemen — or as he did in a heap of mud, in the brambles, on the threshold of the salon, etc."

"Well then, he's got the fall-downs!" Uncle intervened in the conversation.

"Oh, not that, Excellency. Epilepsy is primarily a physiological disease, whereas morbus sedatorius is solely psychological; of course, at Your Excellency's distinguished suggestion, it could be named, popularly, 'the sit-downs,' hallelujah!"

"To be sure, there you go, he's got the fall-downs," mumbled my mother's brother.

"May it please you to understand: falling sickness and sitting sickness are diametrically opposed —"

"To be sure, there you go, aren't I telling you he's got the fall-downs?"

"It's enough to make one tear his hair out!" cried the affronted scientist, clutching at his bald pate.

"That's all a bunch of mumbo jumbo!" my brother jumped into their conversation. "He can't stand, hey! hey! his own two feet — no character — a spiderweb — nix, nix!"

"Quite right, Excellency!" Doctor Trottelhund replied to him kindly. "His Excellency is really lacking equilibrium of temperament — and this is certainly a precondition of his disease; to be sure — another ingenious idea has dawned upon me: not only a precondition, but a direct cause: the awareness of psychological instability evokes in the poor wretch such a lack of confidence in himself, in his physical strength, that he is forced to sit down, wherever it may be."

"In short, he's got the fall-downs!" concluded Uncle. — And now the fat scientist chimed in:

"But how do you explain, my esteemed colleague, all the other manifestations of His Excellency's disease by sitting sickness?"

"By a total disruption of the nervous system, totally con-comitant and incidental to sitting sickness, which is not, however, the most immediate *efficiens* of these sicknesses, my respected col-league Biersterne."

"My renowned colleague, with all the respect I have for your mind, I must say that your entire hypothesis is worthy of a down-right idiot. Even a sophomore wishing to avoid flunking Latin would not permit himself to create this 'sedatorius' term of yours. Mine is a hundred times more apposite. Gentlemen, our patient is suffering from the idée fixe that he is a four-legged animal. It is thus far unclear to me whether it is a gorilla or a baby calf or a dog or an elephant or something else. That is why he most prefers to sit on the ground; that is why he sleeps in stables, why he barks, why he bites and kicks policemen; in order to imitate animal devoracity he ordered that an enormous caul-dron of beans and vegetables be cooked for his lunch; in order that all his behavior reflect completely the animal character of brutality, he shouts those obscenities everywhere!"

"Well, and haven't I been telling you he's got the fall-downs?" — For a moment there was silence; no one can imagine the impression Uncle, by this unprecedented tenacity in his assertions, made on everyone, and how he absolutely stunned them all; but that does not mean he meant anything by it. I think he does it only because he has no forehead.

"My renowned colleague, Biersterne," Doctor Trottelhund finally cried in a quivering voice, "with all my respect for your intelligence, I must declare you to be an absolute cretin. — E.g., it is known that His Excellency has shouted that he is an elephant and the German Emperor. How do you explain the latter with your bestial hypothesis? Do you perhaps have the courage to assert that His Majesty is a quadruped? Or —"

"Mumbo jumbo!" my brother piped up in the middle of all this, fortunately — otherwise they would have come to blows. "It's no sickness, — he's got no legs of his own, hey, hey, nix! He's like laundry in the wind, like a sparrow — fltt! chirp, tweety-tweet-tweet, peep, peep, peep!"

May God fell you, O sparrow! A fine general the emperor has entrusted with the lives of his soldiers! . . . But I must stop now, that scoundrel has poured mercury into my arms as well, and the lines on the paper are jumping back and forth into my eyes like the rays of Aldebaran, hey, hey! I'd like to add something brilliant here — — hocus pocus kootch-kootchy koo — —

Ach, ach — I want peace — peace — — eternal peace — —

July 10

Today for the first time I went out into the garden of the sanatorium. Today for the first time I am writing again. — Oh, I have not known until now that the sun is actually a charming young lad and that the gray earth is a land full of fairy tales. That the azure and the air are more intoxicating than wine! That the rustling of leaves is nothing other than the most real, kind whispering, for me alone, of small, graceful spirits, mischievously concealing themselves beyond matter. I have not known what the feeling of freedom was, the longing for flight into the infinite, the final, tingling radiance of bliss. I knew nothing before. O Omnipotent One, do not let me, as You have up till now, merely suffocate beneath a black mountain of suffering! . . .

Like a white, magical dream, the present wafts about me, like a blue dream the past ebbs away. The late-afternoon sky is without a single little cloud; as is my soul. Although — there, there in the north a small, bluish thundercloud rises, ominous and yet so sweetly alluring. It is the Daemoness . . . But today I am not afraid even to utter her name; thinking of her, I shed tears, a delightful icy chill goes coursing through my body . . . O God-Liberator, grant that this day may last forever. — —

July 24

I am feeling very well. Tomorrow I shall leave the sanatorium. If only I feel as well when free as I do here, in a prison, though a rosy one.

I have hardly thought of Helga at all since the thirteenth of May. Neither during my illness nor in my convalescence. It is merveilleux. I explain it by the fact that she is no longer persecuting me; that she has left me alone. Or that she is no longer allowed out of hell.

She was transformed into a paradoxical dream for me. It is now over. Even a goat's got to kick the bucket . . . All my craziness has drifted away. I am as fresh as a newborn . . .

Back at Saustein. Again I hear the rumbling of those infernal gullets coming from the garden. It reminds me of her; too strongly. That is why I am leaving first thing tomorrow. But I am writing Hagenbeck about the provision of giraffes, buffaloes, and hippopotamuses. If only they would eat up those confounded felines! — I think of her constantly. When I was lying in a state of delirium, I had such dreams about her, I tell you . . . Stupid, of course. I shall relate them while I'm able.

First dream. While fast asleep, I unexpectedly heard a mysterious, most frightening roar. As if all the oceans of the world, compressed into a small area, were storming at once. As if trillions of the damned were simultaneously howling their eternal, unbearable torment. It defied description, although it soon subsided. And I was suddenly marching along a dark, bluish plateau. Everything there was horribly blown apart — a landscape laid waste by the largest modern battle is nothing next to this. And in the midst of this chaos I saw a piece of ground beef. It was no larger than a cat. "It is She," I uttered to myself. And out of that ball-shaped lump there actually came a thin cry, as if a newborn kitten were meowing. "She has lost the decisive battle; there is nothing left of her except hamburger." And although I should have been happy that I was rid of her, I burst out crying, howling like a jackal . . . After that, I don't know what happened.

In the second I saw the Ragamuffin, tall as a tower, carrying her by the scruff of her neck like a puppy. But she was still hamburger, although I could make out her little head and legs. He threw her into a deep pool of liquid dung; "drink it all up, now!"

he ordered. "Man of mine, how can anyone stand it?" "A human being cannot; but a god can. If you drink it all up, you will die; if you die, you will be alive, you will be a god!" "But it can't be done, it can't be done!" "It will be," cried the degenerate, and he submerged her entire head in the dungwater. And she drank; and drank; and she writhed. Suddenly, she jumped up. "You tyrannical brute! It could be done even without your dungwater!" And she shredded his face with her claws. "Can't do it," he chortled. "Without drinking this dung it's no good at all. Each gulp of dungwater you drink will become wine. Gods drink only dung! But it must become sweet before it changes into wine!" Again he submerged her head. But she slipped away from him at once with a ferocious yell — and they shredded each other with their claws like two cats, he laughing loudly, she crying desperately. And as a roundish lump they moved further and further away from me, until they disappeared.

The third. "Helmut, man of mine! I want to make love to you!" Thus rang her voice from afar. After an extremely long time she came into view. But she was a sheep. "I had to transform myself so that I could — —" And she took hold of me somehow or other with her strange little legs, pulled me onto the ground — and, well, we did it — —

July 26, in the train

I shouldn't have written about those dreams yesterday. Now I'm thinking of her again constantly. It's not so horrible, on the contrary, it's almost pleasant, lascivious . . . In spite of that, this first step may lead back — into the old abysses. — I won't even let myself think of her! I'll drive away every thought, every second! —

Yet in fact, these dreams should make me happy. If she had won that decisive battle, no devil could withstand her! Much less I, who have had to bear the brunt of it all! She wanted, the little vixen, to become God, keeping her hatred and vengefulness safe in her back pocket. But after all, that would make her — Satan! And — Christ the Lord! what would lie in store for the one who stuffed a certain sock between His teeth, after first knocking them out with a knife handle . . . My teeth are chattering . . .

Thank God she's over that; I wonder where else she's meddling! And now she's certainly back in that scarlet hell, being tortured until she cries hallelujah . . . They've surely pulled the reins in on her . . . Perhaps she can't get out of hell at all; she can't get to me. That's why she's left me in peace for so long . . . Yet — she did meet with the ragamuffin, he was dunking her in a pool of dung . . . Ah! obviously he's also in hell, he's a devil there and is tormenting her, as he tormented her in life. Yet it's to my great advantage that he wants her to forsake vengeance; she obeys him like a dog. He wants, so it seems to me, that she fall in love with the one she wants to destroy; even when they were on the knoll that time he ordered her to kiss me. Nice of him, I won't call him a ragamuffin in everything; it testifies, of course, to his lack of love for her if he isn't jealous of me.

Yet the most important thing is: the Daemoness, it seems, shall be tormented until she abandons her vengeance . . . and until — that killer of hers — — —. Before, she only had to kiss me . . . Yet now, that's no longer enough . . . , she must fulfill her marital obligations . . . And she, the poor, tormented wretch, is probably ready to do so . . . That's why she came to me as a sheep — —

Oh God, God! . . . what awful thoughts, having — relations with a ghost, even though it's your lawful wife . . . But the thought tickles me . . . How strangely beautiful! . . . What would all the erotic escapades in the world be, next to — this here? Oh, oh! . . .

My special railway carriage is traveling so smoothly I'm writing as easily as if I were at home . . . I would love to expand on this seductive topic, since I'm squirming with delight and horror . . . , does that make me perverse? Do I go in for eighty-year-old geezers, like Messieurs X. Y. Z.?

Am I afraid of her or do I desire her? . . . But after all, just a while ago I said that I didn't want to devote even a moment's thought to her. Yet — I have not written about her, only about my dreams . . .

Everything is going beautifully, just a few more days of peace — and I'll be living it up again like no one has ever done before! —

July 31, evening

I am now living in one of my villas, just outside Berlin. The countryside is beautiful. Flat as a mirror. There's almost no flora here, since the ground is so sandy that it would only be good for grist. But I have had a thousand boxcars of black earth brought to my expansive gardens from the Ukraine. Everything in it grows as if wild. Here I cultivate, actually my gardener does, many rare, exotic herbs. For that reason I was visited today by Count P., the botanical maniac, a gentle crackpot. The confounded fellow . . . he'll even kneel in front of an ordinary little flower and weep over it — — —

At two in the afternoon I was showing him around the garden. The sky absolutely clear. The sun as wild as if it wanted to swallow us up. I couldn't stand it, and could stand that idiot even less. Somewhat violating the laws of hospitality, I shook free of his company and left him kneeling in front of a bud. Small birds, mostly sparrows, were twittering away so hopeful and carefree, the midges teeming so thickly in the air, like snowflakes in a blizzard, buzzing monotonously, hypnotically, like the dreamy murmuring of my garden's fountains. I traipsed about and whistled to myself. The gazebo. "Have yourself a good long nap in this heat, before that crackpot awakens from his slumbers!" I told myself; parting the curtain of wild grapes and ivy, I went inside the gazebo.

It was surprisingly dim in there; I could barely see anything at all. Only after a moment could I make out — Her. She was sitting on the table. Back leaning against the wall. Arms folded on her chest; motionless. Face — horrid. No one, except her husband, would have recognized her. A skeleton. If she had been outdoors, she would have likely been dandelion yellow; but here, in the womb of the dark green walls, impervious to even a single ray of sunlight, where it was darker than a spruce grove at noon, she looked like a watergoblin suffering from jaundice.

Eyes open. She was unblinking — like Odin, her gaze was unmoving. I would have taken her for a corpse, eerily sitting up instead of lying down, if her stomach hadn't been stirring weakly with her breathing.

It was appalling; even so, this time fear did not overtake me. Not even running away like a scared rabbit, I blurted out, without even knowing why:

"My precious wife, please tell me, how have you been?"

She did not reply. It lasted an eternity. Finally there came a horrible whisper:

"Badly."

"But how can that be! After all, you look so joyful, young, and fresh . . ."

An endless silence. — "I am afraid you did not win the decisive battle . . ."

"I lost . . ." followed after a while, as if borne by the wind.

"But by all the saints, you, my wife, lose? Such a fine and hale woman!" —

"They cannot be merged after all: Hatred with Radiance Eternal . . ." drifted out next from the sleeping woman's unmoving lips. "Hatred is black; even the gods are black; God is white. Night cannot enter into Day; a bat could not aspire to be an eagle of the sun. I had hoped to reconcile them. Impossible. It is necessary to love — to love everything; even what is most revolting. Love is the cruelest, most difficult thing of all. Herein, however, lies the Mystery: that which is most revolting is more likely to melt into love than that which is only half revolting — —"

"Am *I* that which is most revolting?" came shouting out of me.

"No longer — not quite — — Don't ask. Let me sleep. Come closer."

And then — I was sitting next to her, and she, appallingly! put her dear head on my chest . . . And seemed to be sleeping; and so was I . . . At least that maniac told me later that he had spent a good two hours praying in front of the flowers — —

"I — do — love — you," I heard sweetly in my slumber. "For the very reason that I find you so unpleasant. At the crucial moment when everything collapsed, I realized that, tainted by hatred, I would not become Radiance. And at that moment Will and everything failed me. Once and for all. I felt myself powerless for all eternity, like a newborn babe. In everything, everything, Everything, one must see the most blessed Radiance and Delight, only One's Own Radiance and Love for Oneself, if a person desires to become the Divine Delight of Radiance and Love —"

And she said much, much more in this vein; but I have forgotten it, the way one forgets dreams. — Then all at once I felt like giving her a little peck. Suddenly I went flying off into the corner. And then she was standing over me — completely changed! Gone was her somnambulistic gaze, the greenish yellow of her face blazed pink, and her former, terrifying voice pealed:

"What do you think you're doing, you mangy old dog?"

"I, nothing — I, nothing — but you were just holding me" —

"I — you? Are you crazy? And what kind of insolence is that, addressing me in the familiar?"

"You — I mean, madam, you were sleeping and confessed your love to me — because you — lost that battle —"

"What are you babbling about? . . . Yet" — as she covered her face, "yes . . . I was just dreaming my ususal dream: I had to swallow a toad: a lifeless, smelly, fat, scabby toad. And I had just bitten into it — —. And now *you're* here? Out, out!" She shouted angrily, as I'd never heard her shout before.

I would have been prompt to oblige her if I hadn't staggered on the sand inside the gazebo. She was kicking me, raging wildly: "out, out!"

"I cannot — please — please . . . I was just in heaven, and you were a sheep there — and now you're sending me back down to hell."

"Just you watch me! Just you wait, you'll be there in no time at all, hey! I'll give you something to worry about, and quick! . . ."

Seeing that she had stopped kicking me, I found the strength to say:

"You — you're still there? Alas! So you haven't won it after all —"

"*It* was lost. But *I* have not lost! Losing only means: winning later. No pain, no gain. The only mother of strength is pain. You look forward to the day when this breaks me, 'straightens me out'; this would have broken a half-pint soul of your ilk a thousand times over! I — have been transformed from flint into a diamond! The more burning my torment, the more burning my thirst for vengeance — on the one who brought this upon me. Either you figure out who it was and tell me the next time we see each other, or all my vengeance will fall, terribly, on you alone!"

And then she very quickly put a veil over her face and parted the green wall. "Wife!" I moaned from the depths of my desperation, "vengeance belongs to God alone. You are like a child who is incessantly beaten because of a bad habit; if he has any common sense, seeing that he will be punished again and again, he'd rather give the habit up. And it is the same with you — there in eternity . . ."

Then, wouldn't you know it, once outside she suddenly chortled almost merrily. "You nincompoop, you nincompoop!" I could still hear. — — —

Almost immediately, an anxious touch roused me from my torpor —

"Have you fallen asleep, my dear friend? . . . That is only natural: in this heat, even the eyes of the flowers are drooping sleepily —"

"Did you just see a lady leaving here, wearing a veil?"

"I didn't see anything."

"Didn't you hear her yelling?"

"I didn't hear anything."

"I tell you, she was yelling like ten jaguars! They must have heard her as far as Berlin!"

"Not me. But I did hear whispering: the whispering of a flower. As if it were human, articulate. It's a pity I don't know the language. Evidently an African dialect. Please, come with me quickly, perhaps you will be able to still hear it; then I shall explain to you in detail to what genus and species the plant belongs —"

Well, I went with him, the fruitcake. He'd be a model trial witness, that one — — —

— — — Let me be, let me be, or I'll go crazy! . . . I tossed vases, paintings, ashtrays out the windows of my room — everything, at the same time shouting, I don't know what — — —

Now I am living in another of my villas. On leaving the first one, I spat on it and trampled the flowerbeds.

There are bars on the windows here. I hastily had double doors put in everywhere. I also have hand bombs. We'll just see what happens after I throw one under her. If I killed you once, girl, what's to keep me from killing you a second time?

Were it not for the fact that before she woke up she began to — — with me, I would have gone mad from fear right then. That memory is sweet as sugar . . .

Surely she knows now who killed her; she must have known it from the start. She was only playing cat and mouse with me.

Sst, sst! there's another rustling in the next room . . . Tap, tap, tap . . . Like my late mother-in-law. But that piggy of mine — she's reaching for the doorhandle — it clicked —. I shouted out my formula; the tapping stopped. But the formula alone is not enough without the Podex romanus. Where to get one? That wretched Kuhmist is languishing in prison. Right after establishing my identity at the police station, they caught her as she was getting ready to leave for Switzerland. "Where do you have the money you wrung out of His Excellency?" they bellowed at her. She told them nothing. She shared my fate. They stripped her, tied her up, and gave her a thrashing. She said nothing, and in the end she fainted. The next day they did the same, until the floor underneath her was red. And at that point she confessed that she had buried it in the pigsty where she fed her hog. They found it there; not one mark was missing. At the intervention of the emperor himself she got a good 10 years.

I would have turned to Willy with a request for clemency, but I am in disfavor. Don't think it was because of my excesses. My deeds had so impressed the emperor that he composed an epopee about them and painted, rather, he commissioned from his personal painter, five works on the following: 1. Sternenhoch slapped by a dead maltster; 2. Sternenhoch befriending a calf; 3. Sternenhoch receiving blessings from a witch; 4. Sternenhoch paying in a dive bar; 5. Sternenhoch on the bench at the police station. What's more, he even composed melodies and sketched out the design for a small cathedral where all these masterpieces would be preserved for all time. He even inquired after my health; and after Helga. Neither he, nor anyone else for that matter, took note of the fact that she had disappeared: it is generally known that, like the Austrian Elizabeth, she always made herself scarce whenever she felt like it, as if she didn't have a husband at all.

I am in disfavor because on the street I exclaimed: "I shall be Emperor of Germany!" Under the lash, Kuhmist confessed that she had prophesied this to me . . . I'm even fearful of assassins

— —

Once again the dragon's maw has opened wide for me. Now I am damned; for good. I feel like cattle being led to the slaughter . . .

But on top of all this there is — doubt. — Why did she laugh like that as she was leaving? Why did she say to me twice "you nincompoop"? — — But the very idea itself is too nincompoopish — —

Oh blessed light of this day! I am saved, once and for all! Something wonderful has happened. I shall die of happiness — O God, how merciful You are, and I — what a nincompoop I am! . . .

Due to my exultation and dancing and laughter, I cannot write any more today.

Well then: After a sleepness night, I went walking in the morning through the fields along a path leading from my villa to a small wood. During my entire stay here I had not yet dared to venture outside the house; until yesterday. "But you're only going as far as the wood," I told myself. For as long as I can remember, I have been horribly afraid of the woods; and my horror has multiplied since that day in December when I saw the Daemoness on the park bench . . .

There was a lowering sky, and yet the heat was oppressive. Vapid thoughts rolled about as if drunk, all objects around me reeled drunkenly.

I was only 50 paces from the wood. I became frightened. "Go back now, while there's still time!" . . . I turned around — and five paces in front of me — She.

I wasn't even that terrified, so phlegmatic have I become. "This is the end . . . Let it be! so much the better . . ." I muttered to myself and sat down, quite slowly, on the edge of a field. "At least when they shoot me I won't fall face down on the ground, smash my nose, and break my legs."

She threw herself on the ground three paces away from me

and lit herself a Virginia cigar. Her face was calm, mocking, and cruel. "Brave, unconcerned, mocking, violent — thus wisdom wants us": these words, supposedly Zarathustra's, occurred to me. She was silent for a long time; and my heart beat more and more forcefully, until I was near fainting. Finally she spoke:

"Today I bring you tidings of great joy. This day marks the end of your afflictions — —"

There was a double meaning in this; but for the moment it escaped me. Pure joy exploded within me. That hellcat, having led me from stupor, the stupor of her hateful hunger for vengeance, into hope, knocked me straight into the abyss.

"Who, then, is my killer?"

"I still don't know — unfortunately . . . I have begun an investigation. Detectives — from Paris, New York. They haven't found him yet. But I have also written Sherlock Holmes. He still hasn't found time to come, but as soon as he does —"

"He won't be needed. I have figured it out for myself."

"But how on earth could you have —"

"His face came back to me clearly . . . It was small as a dog's; beardless; toothless; watery eyes; the look of a carp; a tiny pug nose; an altogether misshapen chimp."

I howled with dread. "Are you still making jokes, Prince?"

Involuntarily, I clasped my hands together . . .

"What are you doing?" she chortled. "Aha! you are rather like that knave, your brother, the general — my killer . . ."

Oh, how my blood boiled over! "Wha-aat?" I whinnied, lightning flashing from my eyes. "Do you think *he* would have dared to carry out such a black deed? . . . Well, of course that scoundrel is capable of anything, just not anything good; he's a savage tiger. I have hated him from my very soul, that sparrow! Tweety tweet tweet —. And he always hated you, my wife! He was opposed to our marriage; he said it was a mésalliance. Now it's all clear to me. But a widower's vengeance, like a lightning bolt, shall pulverize him —"

"Very well. Tell me: what punishment does such a villain deserve?"

"Death," I shouted.

"You have pronounced your verdict. It was you — you!"

I caught sight of her familiar, bluish dagger, coming slowly toward my neck — and my wretched consciousness left me. —

And then — I saw the sky above me. It was quiet as the grave. Absolutely no one nearby . . . I sat up. At this point I saw, behind a nearby shock of rye, blue smoke rising. I got up. The Daemoness was sitting there, smoking, writing something. I wanted to run away. She turned — and burst into laughter:

"Pull yourself together, Prince! Ha ha! How well everything has worked out for me! Cut the comedy, you wretch! I am alive, the real Helga, don't stare like a fish! I didn't croak in your dungeon!"

"Impossible — impossible —"

"You stupid ass! Letting yourself be led by the nose for so long, ha ha ha!"

"But — I saw — you lying — there — dead — in December."—

"You old woman! If you'd had the courage at least to give those clothes a kick you would've heard — the rustling of straw! You could've spared yourself the beans and vegetables, old Kuhmist, the thrashings, the policemen's straps, the madhouse —"

"Lord God, the clothes, the clothes! . . . But — the corpse's stench that was there —"

"Musty air. The stink of your noble ancestors' victims. And perhaps your stink as well."

"Yes — my own stink — excuse me, excuse me. Yet when you came to me — through the keyhole — that time when you whipped me like a horse — or in the washroom —"

"If, in a fever, you saw that sheaf there on your duvet, would it follow that it was not lying here in the field? — I visited you, real, nine times in all. The first time at the court ball; having frightened you there, I disguised myself as a man and went out through a series of rooms; those two pederasts saw me, but they had reason to keep silent. The second time, in December in the forest. The third time, in town with the doctor. The fourth time on Christmas Eve. The fifth time in the park, in March. The sixth time, in the carriage. The seventh time, on top of the cabinet, near the ceiling. The eighth time, in the gazebo. The ninth time — here! — What do I have to do, e.g., with the lady who slapped you, you flunky, when you pinched her behind? With the hallucinations your guilty conscience has created? True, I did have a certain influence on their appearance, telepathically —"

"Oh, wife of mine! you are alive, then? . . . Oh, what happiness, that I am not burdened by the terrible sin of — murder . . ."

"Yes, you are. It's no thanks to you that I managed to escape. Just think what would have happened to you if I were still there today, rotting . . ."

"No, no! Half-mad, I ran into the tower on the second of September, intending to free you, even if you stabbed me on the spot. But — you were no longer responsive . . ."

"Straw won't talk to you. Coward! Couldn't you have at least opened the door?"

"I am a coward, I am . . . So then — you aren't in that — scarlet institute?"

"Everything I told you about that, everything, was made up. A part of my plan: slowly, cunningly, to deprive you of your reason."

"You have succeeded — twice already . . . But — if you don't mind my asking — are you planning on a third time?"

"No! You've been punished enough! It would be too banal to torment further a little worm like you. Nothing would be easier for me than to squash you under my heel — one way or another — slowly or instantaneously . . . But I'll leave it to fate to determine how you, who have been nearly and fatally put under a boot heel, shall be finished off. To live on — that will be your greatest punishment. — But you'll have nothing to worry about from me. Our accounts have been settled."

"Is this only a blissful dream of mine?" I burst into tears. "I still don't understand how it is possible for you to be here, alive . . . How were you able to get out?"

"Well, I'll tell you." She rolled closer to me. "So: —

"When, after you left, I regained consciousness, I began to roll back and forth in the utter darkness, trying with my filthy face to feel out some kind of sharp stone in the wall, to try and cut through my fetters. It was at least 24 hours before I found something suitable. Much longer before I cut through the ropes on my hands and feet . . . Oh, oh! . . . Then, knowing that in old castles there are often secret passages with doors that open only when touched in a certain way, I dragged myself around and around, pressing the walls and the floor everywhere at random . . . Oh, what a job! . . . It took three days. It drove me nuts. Finally, exhausted by hunger, thirst, and mainly by the horrid darkness, having given up all hope, I lay still, as if I had died . . . But eventually, from mere boredom, I started slogging away again — and a moment later, something rumbled in the wall — loosening itself — — — and I staggered into the passageway, blissful as a god — — —." She continued more drily, tersely:

"I climbed down the very narrow, steep, winding stairs. On my behind. For a long, long time. Finally a damp wall blocked my path. I found a hook on it by feeling about, and pulled on it. And once again I saw light.

"Although very weak, the light blinded me. The shadows of the cellar, well-known to me, seemed as bright as the sun's disc. — There was no one inside. I walked through it — the door leading outside was open — I was free. But I returned to the cellar. There were lots of smoked and cured meats, wines, pails of milk and other edibles . . . A hyena that had been starved for a month would not have thrown itself on a sheep more ferociously than I on those treasures — —. Eventually someone began to come near. I slipped back into the passageway, drawing the door shut, and, blissfully happy in my feeling of satiety and salvation as well as — of slight drunkenness, I lay down there and thought, opening the door a crack every now and then, smelling the light.

"And I thought about Revenge. I formulated a hellish plan.

To pretend to be a ghost and haunt you to the point of madness and death.

"Familiar with your cowardice, I knew this: if you dared come into the dungeon at all, it would be enough for you to see, even if only for an instant, my outfit; the patches of color would fascinate you . . . And I took a bundle of straw and a candle from the cellar, returned, miraculously strengthened, to the dungeon, undressed, stuffed the clothes with straw and went back downstairs. And I waited behind the door until the cellar light went out. Other people had been there in the meantime, but there was no mention of the mistress of the castle. People had obviously concluded: she's flitted off to some foreign land, like so many times before. Everyone, without exception, accepted this; only my dear cats in the garden knew the truth — —

"Throwing some sackcloth on myself, I left the cellar. I went through the dark corridors to my rooms. No one saw me. I got dressed, took a good deal of money, left the castle like a spirit and — went to find Him . . ."

She moaned alarmingly . . . "He — had departed . . .; only one day earlier . . ." Yet she immediately continued, cool and terrible:

"You're not responsible for his death. Otherwise, I would take you and —. Since that day I haven't lived, I am dead, do not think that I am alive! . . . I would have killed myself if Revenge had not been smoldering within me. Revenge — the great Preserver of life. It is only thanks to the idea of revenge that I have stayed alive. — But — to squash you like a bug? . . . Ugh! — Over time I calmed down until I became quite placid . . .

"From the beginning I have tracked you and traced your every step. I had detectives. But it ultimately revolted me, as does everything in this world. — I want to finish this delightful life peacefully, tamely, in seclusion. I now have my home in a certain village, raising rabbits, writing a comic play, and perhaps I will also become an actress. But my money is dwindling: — Prince, in fact, I have come here today to pump you for money! It's like this: I'm asking you to give me 5000 marks a year — don't be startled! I don't need more! and when I become a famous author, actress, and big-time rabbit-breeder, I will renounce even that."

I was melting in a dark, consuming bliss. "Helga, for the king's sake — 5000 — — 5,000,000 I will give you! If you knew, if you only knew! You don't know what I've been through —"

She laughed, so sweetly and kindly — — she waved her little hand — and shuddered. The wretched woman! what she herself has had to suffer! . . . And she began to leave.

"Helga!" I could not let her leave just like that, "is it even possible? . . . Yes, everything, just as you explained it to me, it's so natural, everything clickety-clacking along beautifully. And yet — is it not a dream, that — you are alive?"

She stopped. "What a nincompoop you are! That nonsense still hasn't gotten out of your head! — Besides — you can convince yourself anytime you like by going to — the tower. You murdered Elephant and Lion, you beast: but just try bringing a real lion with you and all the rest of them from the garden! I guarantee they'll follow you like dogs and won't touch your revolting body!" Once again she made to leave, in the direction of the forest.

"Helga — do you mean — that we shall never — see each other again?"

She turned her head around while walking and called out, in a voice so strange:

"We shall, we'll see each other once more!" —

I remained sitting. After a moment I looked up. She was no longer there. She had disappeared into the forest — — —

Hey hey! 5000 marks a year, Lord in Heaven! That's what's left of all these horrors! . . .

I'm so blessedly happy that it's got me bouncing off the walls, I'm a god, I'm a god — — —.

August 12

In Berlin. Happy. I'm drinking again, and kissing and rejoicing. Oh, what beauty, to be rid of a terrible, suffocating burden, the kind a resigned person is used to being inseparably attached to his whole life long! Whoever has not known this feeling has not known happiness, has not lived.

The only thing I don't understand, though I'm laughing now, is how I could have been such a complete idiot for so long. To think that a corpse could keep shadowing me, all the time, not for mere chitchat, but for all this! A normal ghost has at least enough decency to pop up all at once and then go poof, like a spark jumping from the furnace.

Eulenburg is ringing for me . . . Beauty! Glory! Praise be to the All-Loving God and to Bacchus the Liberator!

August 13

Certain doubts have begun to nibble away unpleasantly at my joyfulness, like a mouse beneath the floor . . . Do I have absolute certainty that last time she was here she wasn't just — a ghost? . . . She said she had made up everything having to do with the red institute, etc.; who can guarantee that she didn't make up everything she told me the other day about her escape from the dungeon —? . . .

All kinds of things lately are difficult to explain — if she is alive; but if she's dead — it doesn't make it any easier.

And then, that time in the forest, she disappeared too quickly . . . She would have had to run like a horse. Of course, I was lost in a dream, out of my head, and a person like that easily loses his sense of time. Perhaps she also hid herself behind the shock of rye . . . ; she's full of tricks — —.

I really don't know anything for certain any more. It is — an appalling fact . . . What ghastly thing has shaken me so? . . . Hoo, hoo, hoo —

But this is all absolute nonsense. She is alive and won't bother me ever again. Probatum est.— The one thing I don't like is that she has become a rabbit-breeder, a writer, and an actress. Although it's commendable that she's putting her talents to use with rabbits instead of with jaguars, it's no passion fit for aristocrats. If she raised horses, or dogs, at least! Yet my wife wants to become an actress? And even a writer? God, spare me this shame! I'll have none of it! . . .

Yet my thoughts keep coming back to the absurd . . . There is a way out: to go back to the dungeon. Either I will find straw there, or — — but I dare not even think of that "or" . . .

Moltke is ringing for me. — — Why did that sound like the pealing of a death-knell? . . .

Written in the evening. Perhaps now I'll manage to write something rational. I must work quickly, however, since I shall soon be enveloped in darkness once again. At the moment, I am unusually lucid, as often occurs when the darkest night is swallowed by a lightning flash.

Nothing else has happened, except that I had a dream today — or was it a vision? or reality? It was all that and still more. It was a flash of hell that I had swallowed, that had swallowed me — — At midnight I awoke from the dream — or was it an awakening only in a dream dreamed about an awakening? But that's beside the point, because —: I saw her next to the bed, on the floor. Bound, half-naked — blood and muck. In her horrible, skeletal, insensible face rolled the eyes of a corpse, her lips were bitten to shreds, and even her knees, which had served her as sustenance, were gnawed to pieces. She was writhing and screaming unimaginably, from the depths of hell — and I heard the words: *"Fourteen days,* like nights to me, I waited for you to have mercy — and you had none . . . I died there — —"

The main thing in all this is: the terrifying flashes of lightning, the terrifying thunder that were this phantasm and its words. But it's impossible to express; in the face of a dream like that, or whatever such hellishness is called, Goethe himself is an impotent idiot.

It all lasted but an instant; yet this would have been enough to tear arteries and brains less weakened than mine to shreds. — The lightning flash went out. And when I came to, a kind of new, unfamiliar night lay above me . . . Madness. Only now do I understand; I am really in the grips of — — —.

However — perhaps it isn't the end just yet. After all, I am concious, at least for the moment. In my night, through the whole of this day, a tiny little star has been twinkling . . . ; it twice has become as brilliant as a meteor. I recall that these moments are known as lucida intervalla. As I write this, I even feel myself to be an extraordinary radiance, a warrior, such as I have never been before. Nil desperandum; I have even become, as you can see, a Latinist on top of everything else, like a schoolboy. Would you believe that I've put up such a good front no one has noticed my lunacy? To this end, I have shut myself up all day long. This is proof of my healthy instinct for self-preservation. To arms! . . . Yet, ha! the night is closing in on me again, from all sides. — Pull yourself together! I've got to hide these papers in the wall, quickly — — Although — there was something else I wanted to — something —

I know. To the dungeon! Come what may, it must be! I see it clearly: herein lies my salvation, even now! Real certainty can still, though I'm already flying into the abyss, catch me! And it alone! — First thing tomorrow, to — Rattentempel!

Agh — Elephant — Lion — I don't have you with me! . . . There are no other dogs besides you, no other friends of mine in the world; I — am your killer — I'm paying dearly for my miserable deed — and so what — what — night — lie down — —

August 15

I made it to Rattentempel without any mishaps. I didn't have any particular lucida intervalla today, yet my night today was not all that black . . . it was almost pleasant. Though I bark and bay, bite a little and butt about like a goat, I still can't keep myself from laughing.

And do you know why? Because I am saved! Once and for all!

My salvation, you see, is the Podex romanus. Go into the tower to determine the truth? Nonsense! That won't do! Today I went as far as the blue room, but that alone frightened me so much that I ran out, leaving a cloud of dust in my wake, screaming. What would happen if I peeked inside those clothes . . . ? Rubbish!

But the Nut! And I will have it, though Esmeralda's in the clink. Do you know what I found today, faithful Christians? I was walking through the castle garden today — and all at once a frog jumped out underfoot —. I looked — and what did I see? Right where it had been sitting, there was a quill! Very nice; similar to a hen's. I ran after the frog as if it were beautiful as a maiden's smile, but I'll never see it again. Yet inasmuch as it had lost a feather, it was obviously beautiful as a maiden's smile. Clearly it was a queen frog that, startled, shed the quill that grows from its rump once every 100 years.

Hurrah! I have the rarest component of the Podex romanus! and my energy shall provide the rest — What about — the tower — rubbish! . . . I have quite forgotten about all that. The tower — what a joke!

August 16

Today my actions were worthy of Frederick the Great. First thing in the morning, I wrote Hagenbeck to send me gorilla tears, for millions if need be. Then I sent for a glazier. "Hey buddy, would you prepare a glass trap for catching the rays of the planet Aldebaran?"

I bellowed at him. "And provide me with the sweat of a diamond the day after that? You're a glazier, you lowlife, glaziers have diamonds for cutting glass!" "Excellency, I don't know how!" he stammered. — "You Sauhund," I yelled, "and you call yourself a glazier? Either you get me both of them by tomorrow, or else I'll hand you over to the emperor to be quartered and hung by him personally." — "Excellency — I'll — do it" — he gabbled, shuffling toward the door, and he quickly made tracks.

So I knew I had taken care of the planetary rays. Then I went to look for viper droppings on a fern. In the castle garden there are ferns growing beneath the dwarf pines. — And soon I saw a small, whitish patty, a little like sparrow poo. There was no doubt that I had found the third ingredient as well. — I had the viper droppings, I had the frog's quill, and I had Aldebaran taken care of — and I would be surprised if anyone dared say that the future German Emperor would not get the gorilla tears out of that miserable Hagenbeck. Hoorah! I am saved!

August 17

Most holy God! What a madman I was yesterday! I shudder at the recollection of it all . . . I am being watched. To begin with, the glazier told others about me. But they won't dare, the slaves, go to the authorities. They've surely already gone to my relatives; and they're the ones who'll have it done. They would have done it a long time ago, if I weren't so precious to Willy . . .

It is noon. Since early morning I have felt almost normal. And something new, so sweet, rather white, is pecking its way out of me — —

Pereat Podex romanus! My sole protection is: *the tower!* If there is straw there, I know that I'll be cured of my madness, even if I'm in a loony bin, and even if the most celebrated psychiatrists in the world are treating me! If instead of straw I find — — something else — —. Let that corpse jump right on top of me! or let the live one snickering away in the corner stab me all over! Better to end this horror than a horror without end . . .

I'm going there right now, without delay, to the tower!

Before midnight

Hee hee hee! I was there. In the tower, that is; not in the dungeon, of course, heh heh heh! I opened the first door; but the second was so rusty and ugly that I started to scream and ran away, not stopping until I reached my bedroom. Only an hour later did I remember that I had left all the secret doors open. And, take note, I went right back and closed every one of them. It all went quite easily. I was like a sleepwalker. I'm annoyed that I didn't go inside. Something is pecking, pecking . . .

August 18, one o'clock in the afternoon

Although I was crazy again yesterday evening, since early morning today I have been having a lucidum intervallum. Do you know why? Because I'm plastered. I happened upon the ingenious idea of deceiving all the riffraff around me by being constantly three sheets to the wind. Insane as insane can be. That's how I fooled the cops, though it left my rear end smarting. And that's how I'll fool that entire, wretched guard of my relatives!

They're already holding secret meetings. My brother the

general is here, and two female cousins, the clucks. But what are they going to get out of me anyway? I can't stand up, even on all fours, and all I do is shout "Wacht am Rhein."

I certainly couldn't get to the tower now, even if I — whathaveyou — were aflame with longing for her, as if for — a lover. And — you know — I am aflame — with what? mainly with slivovitz, then with fear, and then also — with a longing of some sort — for my other half . . . — She's surely drunk, too, like me, hee hee! Something's pulling me there, pulling — —

But I won't get there this way. I shouldn't drink so much. Because, what's the use, I've got to go there! The Podex is rubbish. Only the tower is wise — wise — and I'm sozzled — sleepy — — amen.

Before midnight

Another luci — lucid — —. But I'm not plastered. Though I don't feel like going to sleep yet either. I just have to throw up.

Well, it's all over. In the evening, while I was sleeping off a hangover, the entire wretched guard, along with three "aristocrats from Baden," reeking of erudition, visited me in corpore. They had organized a banquet. I was and wasn't a lunatic; it depends on how you look at it; at one moment lunacy can seem like reason, at another, reason seems like lunacy. Dreaming is lunacy, as it ought to be, and yet it is half of what a person is. In every way, I had more sense than the whole of that rabble about me. I told myself that I'd start behaving like any normal Johnny, and to this end I remained stubbornly silent and kept right on eating. They didn't get a word out of me, although they wanted to, terribly. When I just couldn't keep my words down any more, I went into the bathroom and threw up. — Oh, no one can put up a better front than a lunatic, and no one knows better than a lunatic that he is a lunatic! Those who think that a lunatic shouldn't know about his lunacy are the biggest lunatics of all. That is the brazenly conceited prejudice of idiots who believe they have an exclusive lease on the mind — and instead of thoughts, their heads are full of shit, and so they condemn everything that isn't shit. Lunacy is only sound reason — dreaming — true reality; — Death — True Life; "life" — just cretinous raving. Come, O Death! . . . Excluded from life, made bright with Suffering, already drunk with Your sweet, suspected wisdom, longing for You . . . Perhaps in Your embrace I'll no longer have legs like a baker, a tiny pug nose . . . , — and there in You perhaps She will — love me . . . —

— After dinner, however, I couldn't keep it up any longer. My uncle began to squabble with my brother over which month was more sultry: July or August? He said July, and substantiated this with the fact that this year he'd soiled more underwear in July than in August. "Mumbo jumbo!" cried my brother, waving his hands like the wings of a small sparrow to whose little beak its elders were bringing tiny worms; "August! what's August! but jackdaws! jackdaws! In August they fly high above the tower, hey, hey! ever so high, wishing to escape the earthly heat — into the ether — higher, higher! August, I say! What's underwear! . . . But the jackdaws, hey, that's another cup of tea, boy! Mumbo jumbo!" By this point I could no longer restrain myself and spouted: "Brother, you scum, aren't you ashamed to be contradicting your illustrious elder? You're as much a fool as those jackdaws of yours, but you ought to have some respect! Is this how you keep the fourth commandment? Honor thy father and thy mother! For your uncle is the same as your father and your mother — yes — he gave birth to you in travail and nursed you —." A silence like the grave descended. All the faces of that wretched guard flared up with joy, and turned to the aristocrats from Baden . . . I know now, and I knew right away, that I had said something deranged; my words did not go unnoticed, agh! among the idiocies of my brother and uncle! . . . But it had already happened — and now other things happened as well. E.g., for a long while, underneath my shirt, I poured wine by the spoonful on my chest while booming at the same time: Deutschland, Deutschland, über Alles —.

In short: I was pronounced in no uncertain terms by the aristocrats from Baden a lunatic, and overheard the quiet words: "Tomorrow, right at sunrise —."

You think you'll cure me there, you madmen! Until you've gone through what I've been through, don't you go sticking your stupid fingers up inside me! It's already asinine enough when someone talks about alcoholism without ever having experienced it to the final stages; how much more asinine when someone talks about madness without ever having had the least whiff of it! . . .

Never have I, a madman, had such a clear mind as at this moment. Only now have I become a true philosopher. And all because of: my longing for You, Daemoness! Incomparable You! Alone among women! Most Miserable You! . . . How unworthy I was of You! What insolence of me to make You, wife of mine — a cripple! . . . It is right that I suffer for this. A stupid lamb,

blinded, took a Tigress for a wife — and a ravenous one at that
. . . It could not have turned out otherwise . . . — Purify me,
set me right, edify me, Helga-Daemoness! Make a Lion of this
lamb! — —*

August 19 at 1 a.m.

In my enthusiasm, as I was writing those last words, I saw all at
once by the wall — Him — Hers. Arms crossed on his chest, he
grinned insouciantly like some god, and at the same time, without even looking down, was kicking a body that was writhing
beneath his feet, its hands bound. He was kicking it to the rhythm
of a waltz, such that it rumbled like blows to the largest drum
imaginable; and then he kicked the body over to me. "Look at
it, how beautiful it is now!" he roared. And She, from the crown
of her head to the soles of her feet looking as if she had just
been modeled out of chilled blood — bounced up, embraced me,
kissed me — "But You'll throw me over again in an instant, toad
that I am!" I yelped. "No — for you are a Seraph! and I was
blind!" came the sublime whisper from within her . . . And —
yes! all this time, a stunning white light blazed behind me . . .
and, at that moment, it exploded like a sun and engulfed me, Her,
Him! —

Yet it was not a vision like the ones I was having before, such
mortally clear ones. Mists enveloped the apparition entirely, as
if it were only an image from an overactive imagination. But I
feel: that this is an Omen of something enormous. And it shall

---

* The ink here is splashed as if the penholder fell from the author's hand onto the
paper.

come — it shall come this very day. It is meant for me, the most abject of men, as if I were omnipotently dictating orders today, like fate itself! —

I am overjoyed. No longer human. I would go into the tower immediately, but my limbs won't allow it. After the light of sunrise, I'll be there. By then it will be easy. Whether it be straw, or rotting slime, crawling with worms: it's all the same to me now. *Everything* is alive; Nothing does not exist! . . . — And everything that is, is God. She refuses to understand that a toad is nothing but a pure, golden, heavenly cloud . . . That is something no one understands but I, the lowest of worms, elevated by the most unprecedented suffering, having attained Reason by way of Madness. A wren that has soared over the eagle, over You, poor Helga, steeped, because of your arrogance, in a greater night than I, a pathetic little mole; the more tormented You are, the more divine, the more God demands of You! . . . You will not liberate me; I, a humble madman, will liberate You — O Most Proud, Most Afflicted, Holy, Goddess mine! . . .

Order a reveille! Now it'll be the easiest thing imaginable, mere child's play, pure delight. I am the Other, I want Death, for I want, in Eternity, You, O Daemoness! — — —

August 19, four-thirty in the morning
For three hours I slept soundly. I was woken, miraculously fresh, by the reveille. No longer my former, abject soul: a heavenly power enlivens my body. The Morning Star is shining, the pallid dawn of the east begins to redden murkily.

Am I now mad? I certainly am! And completely so! as you,

the folk below me, would call it. Otherwise I am — the most luminous person on earth. All of the radiances of Eternity, approaching me thunderously, blaze bright within me — but you, you subterranean moles, are utterly blind to them. Is this Dream? . . . But little is said by that . . . In a dream, after all, everything is somehow mixed up, in a waking state, of course, still more, in me now, simply nothing! — My soul has become superterrestrial refulgence. But you, chiropteran humanity, born of darkness, are naturally forced to consider my Day an accursed night. I am not awake, I am not dreaming, I have lost my reason, I am not mad — — I am simply — there — There. Through suffering the lowly worm Sternenhoch has become Übersternenhoch!

"Behold me," says the Virgo Maria, "and say which of your pains is equal to mine?" Suffering has taken me, humble, called for that very reason, and elevated me so that I might ultimately triumph over all the Caesars — even over You, titanic Woman, even over You — You who are Hers — Unknown One! —

The sunrise is already blazing intensively, and the Morning Star dying within it. It's time — —

I am impelled to add: For nothing in the world would I now take you with me, Lion, Elephant . . . Forgive me, darlings, for I am deathward bound! . . . In my entire life, you were the only ones I ever killed. Not that I killed Helga! She was killed by God . . . But could she still be alive? Perhaps only straw will be there after all . . . But how ridiculous it all is! . . .

To the tower, without delay! Hey, hey! Black clouds are rolling in from the west toward the sunrise, the lightning has clamored, the Voice of Heaven has roared. Roar, O heavens, just as you did then, exactly a year ago to the day! The rays of the sunrise fade beneath the wild thunderclouds, beneath the wild lightning flashes, the morn is become night . . .

I was sleeping in the blue room. Guards are stationed both in the room next door and in the corridor. I've got to be as quiet as possible. But I'm as clear-sighted as a sleepwalker.

— That's the way — that's the way —. The wardrobe moved aside without a sound, the doors, opened — the wretches didn't even stir. The lantern, lit. Thunder and lightning raging. Off I go. To You, my Wife — in Eternity! There this miserable worm will be — eternally Yours!

O God, I know You shall be merciful to Your worm! — —

III

Here end the notes of the unfortunate, most excellent prince. But perhaps we ought to contrive, on the basis of his ante-mortem, its language muddled and yet at the same time transcendentally lucid, what happened in the tower. —

He skulked into the tower and climbed the stairs. "I have left both doors open," he recalled; "if they enter the blue room, they can follow right behind me. But that's ridiculously irrelevant; ridiculous and irrelevant is everything, All."

We shall not endeavor to give a more detailed account of his mental state. Certainly not because it would be "inartistic," or because it should derive completely of its own accord from the final pages of the diary; only because it is beyond the scope of human representation, whether artistic, philosophical, scientific, or any other sort. Art is wretched, like all things human. Whether by artistic or other means, one can only convey the lowly, the human, and barely tolerably at that. Not a Great Mystery. The prince proceeded toward the Daemoness poised between Dreaming and Postmortality; for one who is in a state of "wakefulness," the Dream is almost inconceivable, After-Death completely so. Sternenhoch's Lunacy became Superlunacy, which is Eternity and All. The earthly lay far below him. A moment later he, the most abject moriturus, became a god. — And perhaps "forever" —.

He opened the first door to the dungeon, — slowly and with a smile. He smelled something . . . "The smoke of a Virginia cigar," he said to himself, "hers. Well of course, what else could I have expected . . . Everything is tremendously beautiful. And She most certainly mine in eternity. — Sst! . . . A rustling — from within . . . Well of course."

The key made a ghastly scraping sound in the door, red from rust. And the prince saw the dungeon illuminated, not by his own dim, puny lantern, but by another, standing on the ground — — and then by some kind of weak, mysterious white light. The roaring of diaphanous lions rumbled more and more horribly; the old tower quaked.

And the rose and green spots — were not to be seen. But in the place where they had been was something white. He drew closer. A woman's garment, snow-white. A face covered with a white handkerchief, pressed by white hands. And the whole thing was trembling and twitching and writhing like a ghost. — And beneath it — something rose and green . . .

"She was lying on the straw! Naturally, why would she have lain on the stone! She came here from the cellar. She is alive after all. It almost makes me sorry. It weakens the magic. But — nonsense! Alive — dead — they're both the same. Dead is alive,

alive is dead. The world is merely a living corpse; even a tiger in its magnificent leap — only a galvanized cadaver!"

He knelt beside the woman in white. "Helga!"

The white body stopped trembling and for a long time did not stir.

"Helga, is it You, my wife?"

The body writhed, moaned, and did not speak.

He tenderly removed the handkerchief from her face. "No, no, for God's sake!" roared an inhuman voice. "You shall be damned, and I as well! I cannot look upon you! . . ."

He sat down beside her and waited patiently. "What if it is not She?" the thought occurred to him narcotically. "Did she send another woman here? But what does that matter. All women are — She." — —

"I have come," he could finally hear, in a monotone — "out of curiosity. To determine whether today, this very day, you would have sufficient courage to come here. I have been informed of everything; in a quarter-hour they'll put you in a straitjacket; and I know that you don't believe I am real."

"So you are really alive, then?"

"Only your bad conscience, terrified to the point of madness, could have any doubt on that score. Listen: only the courage with which you cast me in here impressed me somewhat and diminished my aversion toward you. And today, seeing that you have been so fearless in coming, I have respect for you. And in a woman this can intensify to the point of love . . . I think that now I could bear you quite well. Prince, I have really come today in order to propose humbly to you — marital cohabitation unto death . . .

He is dead; I, disappointed by life, blasé, spleenish, without means or support. My financial outlook is atrocious, my rabbits all died suddenly, and I have come to realize that I have no artistic talent. And that those five-thousand marks annually would simply not last me. I would like to be a princess again in the eyes of the world. My one goal now: to be a great lady. If you will accept me in mercy, I will be a model and obedient wife in everything."

"I will do everything, Helga, that you desire. But what you have said is unseemly — No: even this is beautiful; everything is simply beautiful, everything indifferent." — —

— "You are speaking unusually wisely today," — escaped after a while from beneath the handkerchief. "You are somehow different. — I love you — — — and I wish for us, here, before you go — temporarily — to the loony bin — to consummate our second marriage — here, here — in *this* very place!"

And not moving her hands from her face, she embraced him with her bare legs and pulled him to herself. He submitted, but it was not Libido, unless a metaphysical one: kissing *all* — and solely for that reason, Her as well . . . —

As soon as his hands touched her cheeks, however, she immediately gave a terrible shriek . . . And she continued to shriek, like a banshee, drowning out the thunder; seemingly for an eternity —

Suddenly, her shrieking turned to laughter, and the Daemoness's legs again embraced the prince's body, laughing all the while . . . "Come here, oh, come, oh, come! . . ."

And the prince, majestically passive, again fell on the princess . . . — "Come on, come, come on! I will remain faithful, until eternity, through every hell! . . ."

He touched her again. Not with his hands — —. And now the Daemoness remained calm, and only a tiny, hellish chuckle pierced her handkerchief — —.

But — — an instant later —: *"You — You — You —* are here?" — she screamed in horror, not exposing her eyes. "Don't come now, don't come near me now, for the love of God!"

Sternenhoch looked around himself. And in the distance he spied a dim, greenish shadow . . . ; flashing and, at the same time, miraculously more serene than the sun. And it was the enormous figure of a man, with a face that crushed with a mere look, youthful and yet so majestically, divinely mature — —.

— — "Right *now,* you say?" wailed the Daemoness. "But right now — impossible —."

The prince did not hear the reply. — "Impossible that this is the easiest and the sweetest thing there is, you say?" she cried again.

And now Sternenhoch could hear, *without sound,* only in his soul, certain words.

"You yourself are impossible! And the word has become Flesh!"

"Dearest — I cannot!"

"You will! *You wanted at once to break free from him!* Him! Intending to take the most terrible revenge on him, you would be taking the most terrible revenge on yourself!" — —

"Yes, I wanted to! I cannot do otherwise . . ."

"It's over, it's over! It has been won! Simply take hold of your victory!"

"Don't wave that awful whip over me so terribly! I've spent enough time with him — there — there! But Your — more horrible than all the others —."

"Sweeter! Just one last step — hey — hey!"

"Cease! I — will submit myself — to him — and I will not disappear! . . . Do not expose my eyes! Better to put them out!"

"Halfway to salvation! Uncover your eyes! Look bravely!"

"If I look, I will lose the strength to submit, and a terrible hell lies before me as far as the eye can see — —"

"Only if you look will you find the strength to submit."

"To look will be my destruction; semi-blindness is all I can bear!"

"Only bearability is unbearable; and destruction is Radiance. It comes thundering nearer and nearer, suffusing You now, do you not see it, Woman?"

"I don't want to disintegrate, though it be in the All-Radiance. I want to remain Self!"

"The All-Radiance alone is Self. Your Holy Radiance alone is All; your Own Gloriole alone is You!"

"I am afraid of my own white, formless ghost and loathe it; it is sheer Nothing."

"A moth fears the day. O Soul, the most luminous of all and therefore the darkest of all, overabundant Radiance: *You,* who have fallen in love with Darkness, drinking it until you have drowned in it!: Ascend into Your and My eternal homeland! Come to Me!"

And the prince saw the shadow, blazing into a flame ever whiter and more powerful, grow, cut through the ceiling of the cell, and lift His supermajestic, kindly terrible face to the clouds, above the clouds, to the stars, above the stars . . . And from the infinite distances resounded the final, blazing words of a god:

"I, Your husband On High and since Eternity, descended and became human only in order to liberate You from the swamp of Night. It failed — *there;* it was successful here! I sent You into the crimson hells and guided Your every step; as well as those of the one who is awaiting Your Salvation here. Through him have I given You relief, through him am I throwing You Your lifeline in the pool — kindest in my cruelty! . . . Follow me, into the endless Radiance, O woman of Mine!" —

The Voice luminously rumbled to a halt. At its end a shot rang out from the heavens. A lightning bolt struck the tower. And as if the black walls had caught fire by it, a mysterious, white light suddenly multiplied and grew, as a conflagration, ever larger.

But the Daemoness kept her face covered. She tugged several times at her handkerchief but exposed only her mouth. And she began to convulse terribly, as if invisible hands, the strongest imaginable, were shaking her violently.

"That awful, unbearable, inescapable Light penetrates even my closed eyelids," — she moaned. "Hell behind me — scarlet — a white hell before me . . . But *this* is worse . . . And He? . . . only my imagination . . . I will not throw my Self over."

And then the prince spoke, delicately:

"You shall find yourself; You did not have Yourself. We do not have our Selves until we have all, until all inside our Selves melts into love. That which is the most humane seems, to one who, like all people! is accustomed only to cruelty, the most terrible. And that which is the most revolting is the most delicious. My Helga, obey Him! He is one of the greatest gods!"

"Could — you — hear him?"

"And see him as well."

"All of it — only — my — hocus pocus!" she whispered with feminine obstinacy . . . "Well, I'm alive, you lunatic!"

"You are Alive; but in the clothing on which you're lying, there is — no straw! — I do not see it, but I know it — —"

— — "Do you know everything, then —?"

"You came here in order to — submit to me and through this to escape the scarlet hell; today is our last Day. You walked here as if to an execution; dining on dead toads is no small feat; and I was more revolting than a dead toad. Though Your eyes were veiled, when You could not go through with this You fell back on your original intent: to submit to me as quickly as possible — and then to disappear suddenly from underneath me and diabolically leave me, having awakened from heavenly delight, lying on — — a skeleton, covered in terrible slime, worms — —. That was to be the final blow of your revenge. But in that moment — He came. To save You. Not me. For I am no longer afraid. Only now can I make out something under you . . ."

And pulling something awful from under the pink substance — — he kissed it.

"Oh!" she screamed — — and threw off her handkerchief. But her eyes remained closed. "Helmut — no longer does the slighest spark of vengeance smolder within me. Yet that isn't enough — I must also — love you . . . Your spirit is beautiful now — — why is your body so hideous?"

"Perhaps it isn't, dear Helga. Only what we see through the prism of our hatred and revulsion is hideous. Only hatred is worthy of hatred, only revulsion is revolting; no, not even that. You,

Soul, freed of the shackles of the body, do you not yet see this?"

"Oh, disembodied soul! more blind than a mole underground!"

"My Eternal Helga, O sleeping Goddess! I stand on the border between death and Life; lying *behind* me — death; crashing down *upon* me — Life. I see both — by God's Mercy — Your mercy — His mercy — of the Great Unknown. You wanted to destroy me; and you have created from the most wretched of men — one of God's Elect . . . through suffering and insanity. Blessed is my fate. Blessed are all the wounds inflicted by You upon me! Blessed is Your Husband! Thanks to You! I am not a god and Radiance like You; yet I am a reflection of the Divine Radiance, and thus It as well. I am the dirt under Your fingernail, Majestic One; and even that is enough for me: through this as well am I You, You — for Eternity . . . The humblest dog, thrashed to within an inch of its life, is also God. All, even You, is only a reflection of the Divine Radiance — and God Himself is only His Own Reflection —"

"How your voice sounds! Golden and sublime . . . Give me your hand . . . How small and soft it is . . . What — what — what just shivered through me so delightfully? As if I had been touched — by His . . ." She twisted sensually. "Good God — — is that — you?"

And *involuntarily, from sheer longing,* she opened her eyes. The heavens roared for the last time. The white Light multiplied itself hundreds of times. The flames of the lanterns became invisible, like a match-fire in the blaze of the afternoon sun. And every one of the old walls' black stones was a magical diamond of the sun.

— — "Who's there? . . . Oh! It isn't you —. Yet you are — you are — your childlike, childish expression —, but how exquisite you are! A seraph! a god! a sungod — the sun itself . . . Everything around has become radiant with Your diamond light . . . Oh, that I was blind for so long and did not see Your Splendor! Oh, that You were so blind you didn't see it yourself — so that I didn't catch sight of it . . . And how great and powerful you are, towering over the stars, like — Him . . . He and You — you are one! You and I — we are one! In the All-Radiance. O Ocean of My White Light, infinite, which you are in everything! You Perfection, how tender and sweet you are! My Ghost — amorous one! over the primordial Chaos Triumphant, you are Harmony supreme! everything You are not is mere dissonance and pitiful! But the *all* is You, it is necessary only to *see* it; everything is You as soon as it knows it is You! . . . Only now, looking upon You, both majestic and lowly, both divine and humiliated, I know what Divine Omnipresence is, what All and everything and One are . . . Oh, how sweet is Revulsion, how luminous is Blindness! How delightful Pain, beautiful Hideousness, truthful Falsehood — and the Night how supersolar! . . . Oh come, You, My Eternal Beauty — penetrate me, illuminate the Awakened and Saved One — —!"

And she sharply yanked the prince down on top of herself. He felt a pain on his face, but in such a strange way, as if someone else, someone beneath him, were feeling it . . .

The Eternal Light roared about them delectably — — —

Just at the moment, and in the place when and where the stormy, western thunderclouds had set in the east, the sun came out. The castle servants, Sternenhoch's relatives, and the doctors slunk, astonished, into the tower — and into the dungeon. With restrained horror they lit the lanterns. For the prince's lantern had *gone out,* having been drenched with a Higher Light . . . And then they saw him, lying on something rose and green and — — he was moving — — — — — — — — — — — — —

They ran away. Some fainted. They came back. They tore the prince off, while he kept moving . . . he was unseeing, smiling luminously.

One of the servants, who was said to have the gift of second sight, claimed that on entering the cell he saw it illumined by a snow-white glimmering such as is not found on earth; it quickly vanished and in an instant went out in the darkness.

The bones of the arms and legs of a year-old corpse were coiled in ropes. In what was left of the mouth, some filthy rags were found, which science recognized as pieces of sock. The same science pronounced there to be traces of undigested blood in the "stomach" and declared that death had occurred, after about 14 days, by hemorrhaging; the bound woman had bitten to shreds her shoulders, knees, absolutely everything she could reach with her teeth. Otherwise, she would presumably have lived several days longer. She acted thus, asserted the scientists, to alleviate her thirst. In our judgment, however, she ended in suicide. —

In plunging down upon the corpse, Prince Sternenhoch wounded himself on the exposed nasal bone of her face. The Daemoness was amorous toward him even here! — — He died two days later of blood poisoning. Up until the final onset of unconsciousness he was — constantly smiling and happy, like a young man to whom a girl has just confessed her love. He uttered, the super-lunatic, more magnificent thoughts in one minute than a normal intelligent person utters in an entire lifetime. He was delirious, of course; e.g., he confused his wife with the sun's radiance —.

The people standing over him in the hour of his death did not see him with the Eye with which She beheld the true image of his soul, become bright in the dungeon. In spite of this, they did not recognize him and whispered with apprehension: "How beautiful he is!" Even for earthly vision his pathetic baby-face had truly become quite handsome . . . He had thinned remarkably and his nose had become more refined; his transcendentally smiling, thick lips pressed together to form an almost tight line; his forehead had miraculously broadened; and his closed eyes conveyed more than before, when they were seeing . . .

And in the moment when they were closing the coffin over him, his face blazed mystically, as if with its own light, beneath the gaze of the sun. It had not come out the whole day long — and a dark cloud closed over it the instant the lid closed over the head of the Humble Victor.

Then the Goddess sent the cast-off Garment of His Sacred Soul a final, solar kiss. —

MY AUTOBIOGRAPHY

Born August 22, 1878 in Domažlice. Father, a clerk; mildly "well-off." Two brothers, two sisters; all died in childhood. I disliked them all to the point of revulsion, not because they were revolting, but because they had become too close to me. I disliked my parents almost to the point of hatred, although I couldn't complain about them, because they had the audacity to be even closer to me — that is, paradoxically, infamously closer. As a child I hated everyone, every caress made me want to vomit; this idiosyncrasy was especially developed toward all men. It was based on an inborn contempt. If I analyze my memories — it was already in the first few years of my young life that I felt myself and humanity to be like two warring powers; already in my first few years I instinctively belittled the enemy, considering him as nothing. Even then, my will was my basic, powerful characteristic, its flickering brightness penetrating everywhere like the early morning light, ever self-embracing, commanding absolutely everything. It's hard for an adult to live with this, still harder for a child . . . I think it was more developed in my siblings than in myself — that's why they died . . . Of course, with my destiny, I couldn't make a good impression — until I had done a better job of getting my bearings — in the delightful milieu of human society. From the beginning I appeared decidedly ridiculous, funny, bashful, anyone who wasn't like that is just ordinary merchandise. At the same time, I was infernally "self-willed" ("self-will," converse of "other-will," is nothing other than a dark manifestation of the Absolute in the animal kingdom), disobedient, "criminal." I stole for the sake of stealing, and made sport out of breaking windows late at night on the edge of Domažlice, putting rocks on the train tracks, setting sheaves of grain on fire. But as an adult I didn't commit any crimes, because where they aren't required by practical necessity, they're just petty hooliganism — war included. But I also had praiseworthy inclinations: once late at night, for example, as a 12-year-old boy, I remembered that I had failed to give some earthworms I had prepared to a baby bird that I, instead of its parents, had been feeding regularly for some time; I had built a home for it under a bush out in the fields; I slipped out and walked for a quarter of an hour with the earthworms — the bird was dead . . . and I thought I would die over this. Or (tiger) . . . Eh, how stupid childhood is, with all that rubbing your eyes early in the morning! And whoever was "young in their youth" is a fool, a sheep who follows the herd in circles . . . Music gave me my most powerful childhood feelings. If a brass band struck up near me, chills would freeze up my body until it went numb, my eyes would grow dim, and I would grab something to keep myself from falling. Once as a 14-year-old boy I walked for an hour and a half through deep snowdrifts to a village where I knew there would be a funeral with music. From the time I was 10, I would spend whole afternoons by myself in the forests and the fields — and a little later, whole nights. In all my life I have never known boredom — at most, its analogue — and that always in society . . . That herd-like idiocy called school robbed me of at least 30% of my mental powers — that has to be expected, a person will be left with only a fragment . . . I'm ashamed to say that up to the very end I always studied with distinction, and that I always got the highest mark for moral conduct.

At 15, one fateful afternoon, my inner nature, until then sleeping-dreaming, suddenly and terrifyingly awoke under one of its forms: violently forced to think the unthinkable. The rest of the day and the whole night long I writhed in convulsions of thought about ten-thousandths of a millimeter — the necessary consequence of basic "instinct": I am omnipotent — it was impossible to stop my will until my blessed body put an end to it. Since that time it has not left me completely for even a minute; countless times I thought that I — God's most appalling hireling — would submit, for no apparent reason, to 18-hour days of the toughest work there is. Only after I turned 19 did I celebrate a great victory. My convulsions of thought — which I had long considered an illness, as all, at least European, mankind did — were pushed so far to the ground, after unbelievable machinations, that they were no longer threatening . . . The point of my 19 years of permanent writhing, suffocation, and horror was that they bear sweet fruit . . . Only in this way does mankind, does everything in our small universe progress.

To sit at a school desk and be seized by something like this every second — that's not so great. I still didn't have the energy to put an end to that school crap — fate did it for me. In the space of 8 months my mother died, along with my grandmother, aunt, and remaining sister; I systematically disgraced the crosses in the city's environs, caused scandals in church, for lack of bombs threw anarchist leaflets all over the place, etc. —, — until, in the first semester of the seventh form, I was thrown out of all the schools in Cisleithania — because, out of ignorance of history, in a school assignment I called the Habsburgs — I think — a dynasty of swine. The deceased director of the gymnasium, who prosecuted the whole affair so energetically, thus became one of the greatest benefactors I have ever had in my life. I did nothing for half a year, and then I consented to rot further on the benches of a gymnasium in Zagreb. Never was I closer to death than there. After finishing one semester I immediately left for Bohemia, determined not to set foot in any school ever again and not to go in for any kind of career. Two minutes of conversation with my wise father were enough for us to agree on the matter, and since then there has never been any discussion of it between us. I remained in Modřany, where he had bought himself a homestead, for about three years — the ravines and the forests were more my home than my father's house; mostly I was struggling with the primitive question of free will, in preparation for life and death. As soon as I reached the age of 18, I was legally an adult, and received a small inheritance from my mother and sister. I calculated for myself that I could live on it tolerably well for 8 years — I was off by one year — I abandoned, at the age of 21, my father, along with his 24-year-old second wife, who naturally couldn't get along too well with a man in his sixties. I lived alternately in Plzeň, Eisenstein, Zurich, and Landeck in the Tyrol until I was 26. Since

Mrs. Klíma looked after everything necessary for the household, I didn't have to deal with people at all. My only companions were lots of cats. Among visible beings, the things I love the most are mountains, clouds, and cats — maybe women too. My main activities during the years when others acquire experience and start their careers were endless walks deep in the forests, searching for nymphs and hallucinatory chateaux, rolling around naked on the moss and in the snow, and terrible battles with God, Who had decided to live the conscious life of a man . . . In the Tyrol I attained a whole series of necessary preliminary victories — partly since it was there that I got into the habit of smoking. If it weren't for that, I wouldn't be alive today. I decided there to publish, in as concise a form as possible, the main results of my thinking up to then — mostly for financial reasons and against my principle, known to the pre-Socratic philosophers and today paradoxical: to live only for my own self-perfection and, when the circumstances are right, in my old age, to impart to humanity in a single work the outcome of my life. I moved to Smíchov and wrote *Svět jako vědomí a nic* [The World as Consciousness and Nothing] — when I was 26. As I moved to Záběhlice near Zbraslav right after the book came out in '04 and didn't read any newspapers or speak with anyone, to this day I don't know if even a dog so much as barked at it. Only about half a year later did Emanuel Chalupný give attention to it, which had tremendous and favorable consequences for me later. I began to be a little sociable only later on in Zbraslav, at least in the pubs in the evening — what unbelievable things a person's guardian angel pulls on him! Moved to Vinohrady in '06. There I helped myself out by furiously writing aphorisms so I wouldn't suffocate — no company at all. The money ran out. I accepted my father's offer to move back to Modřany (1906). For a year and a half I wrote furiously, only fiction — 2-3 printer sheets every single day, with inexpressible happiness — the deepest part of me would fall asleep for several days at a time, almost as it had slept until I was fifteen; but it was the most pleasant time of my life — in the spring of 1908 I recognized that I was straying from the path, and only then — I'm ashamed to say — did I throw myself completely and full steam into systematic, practical philosophy. The results were enormously delightful, still greater than in my fiction-mongering, but also more difficult and more burning. My father died in the winter of 1909 — just as I was settling up the last debts I owed him — I inherited his buildings. They hadn't been paid off yet, but I could have netted 10-12,000 thousand florins from the sale if I'd only tried. But that very year, and the following, I reached the pinnacle of my life thus far: I found and partially took possession of my Deoessence. Anyone who thinks it possible in this state to devote even five minutes to practical hogwash has no idea what higher spiritual life is. Anaxagoras — who never reached this state — simply neglected his estate. When others advised him to devote at least a little of his time to practical matters if he didn't want to go to the dogs, he said: How could I possibly do that, I, to whom a drop of wisdom is dearer than a mound of gold! — I got about 3,500 florins from the sale. In the winter of '10 moved to Vršovice. Resolution: by the absolute mastery of the intellect to attain fully the Highest . . . 2 years of unprecedented violation of my mental processes — for instance, I would lie in the snow for many hours, numb and in convulsions — A goal that seemed so close, just to reach for it — that was worth the risk of any catastrophe. Unreached; at that time I descended, mainly physically, as low as I ever had till then. Alcohol saved me, rum and undiluted spirits; to this day I've remained faithful to my rescuers. The second half of '12 and all of '13 didn't see me sober even for a minute. But at that time I still managed to keep myself busy with everything possible — I was a novice. At the end of 1913, moved to Horoušánky with Mrs. Klíma and the excellent Mr. Vaniš, whom she married after the war broke out. After that, with quite empty pockets, moved in the summer of 1915 to Vysočany, where to this day, with two short breaks, I have lived in the Hotel Krása, run by the distinguished Mr. and Mrs. Pučálka. After a month's stay in Vysočany, through the offices of Antonín and the engineer Jaroslav Kříž, I became the operator of a steam machine that pumped water from the Cidlina River in Žiželice, and I was running it in no time, although I knew absolutely nothing about it. It went quite well for about two months, then I gave notice and went back to Vysočany. Over a year of unemployment — although you wouldn't have known it — from my outward activity — writing and constant boozing, mostly with that admirable citizen of the German Empire, Franz Böhler. For the first time in my life I began to keep company with certain people every day — mostly with Germans — and later with Jews. In November, became the caretaker for a small factory, completely abandoned. My caretaking consisted only of nonstop drinking. The entire time I was there, the thought never even entered my mind that I might look after the factory. Life was good, I had the biggest apartment in Prague, always had my paycheck all to myself, and light and heating on top of that. The fact that I didn't guard anything was my prerogative, for although I could have stolen a lot of valuable things and sold them, very easily, I didn't steal anything at all, idiot, apart from drinking a bottle of their ether — Absolutely all my jobs till then had been pure farce. A landlord who completely neglected his buildings, a machine operator who didn't have the foggiest idea about the apparatus he was running — seeing to it when it suited him only because he liked to caress it — and there's also my subsequent role: the partner and foreman of an ersatz tobacco manufacturer — limited to boozing with the aforementioned Böhler, my partner. In August 1917 I gave notice at the factory, and three months later "production" began, which lasted till the summer of '18 and brought in about 500 cr., having eaten up about 20,000. After the end of that little war I wrote a bit for the newspapers — thanks to Mr. Kodíček . . . Another farce, just like my two philosophical works and the two *Matthews*. In the summer of '19, a decisive victory both in practice and in theory, since then nothing essential (my opinion) has changed or will change in me; physiognomy incomplete, but it's more or less like in the last 3 dictates of *Traktáty a diktáty* [Tractates and Dictates]. Since then, Dionysius has reigned — which in my case, naturally, has meant that God's god, scilicet Ego, had made him viceroy in me — — It went so far that I suffered the only injury of my life: a fracturam radius sinistris, when I was drunk, running at midnight along the icy roads from Smíchov to Vysočany — November of '19 (October 31). I had more friends than before . . . There wouldn't have been any need to write for the newspapers if this born hermit had seen fit to accept an invitation here and there, if he had answered important letters less than six months after they arrived — as in the case of the inheritance from my father. — How did I spend 1920? . . . Just beautifully, in a state of Self-Embrace, heightened by alcohol and girls, married and unmarried. In May 1921 Böhler moved to Germany — I mention him so often because, in my worst period, he was like Vorsehung fallen from heaven — and maybe my only real friend thus far (next to him, my precious father, who understood me somewhat, was in every respect my enemy. The same goes for his wife). — The summer of that year Dr. Dvořák and I worked on the renowned *Matthew*. The drinking wasn't as intensive as it was with Böhler, but more extensive — every day until the early hours of the morning and beyond, for months. (I boozed the most intensively and exstensively *always alone* — so no idiot could ever say that Mr. X. Y. had corrupted me.) *Matěj Poctivý* [Matthew the Honest] came out on 22.2.1922 — *Tractates and Dictates* about a month afterward. At least *Matthew the Honest* made me some money; *Tractates and Dictates,* except for Chalupný's 1000-crown advance — nothing. The boozing, thanks to the gods! had peaked. Hibernated all winter. The end of '22 — my first battle against it — was grim. The point of '23 (intimissimi aside) was a battle against my life-saver, alcohol, which was then threatening to destroy my life. The battle continues, albeit barely. Otherwise: filled (that year) with collaborations (for the most part) with Dvořák. And from the start of '24 until today (February 21), a convulsively heroic struggle against everything — such as I've experienced 5-6 times in my life. And on the outside, always the same situation. —

My life has been characterized by — on the outside: independence, no "career," the possibility of living for myself in all
circumstances; — I really have always been a hermit . . . Three
phases — on the outside — in my life: first 17 years of crap in
school obviously just can't be avoided if you don't have Nietzsche
for a father, "elevated" to the throne — but except for school, I
was unusually free, thanks to both my wise parents, who somehow understood, surprisingly, what my intimissimum needed;
then: about 17 more years — a time when young men toil away
and scramble after patronage, stinking in slavery at various office
jobs — I was "financially independent," entirely free to live the
life of a hermit — (A certain analogue: Schopenhauer; too bad I
didn't inherit 30,000 Rhenish florins instead of 11,000 Austrian
ones); the third phase: lasting until today: *"financial independence"*
while possessing absolutely insufficient means — totally indifferent
to getting it, constant "negligence," leaving everything to "fate"
or Providence (never asked anyone for money who previously
hadn't told me himself that his cashbox was always open to me;
didn't accept anything from women, in spite of numerous promis-
ing offers and in spite of my being extremely hard-pressed for cash
— I often acted like a millionaire, not knowing if everything
would go bust in four days). And so it went and so it does still
— how, the devil knows . . . A number of my friends (more or
less) were the main reason — and foremost among them are
(alphabetically): Bittermann, Böhler, Březina, Chalupný, Dvořák,
Fiedler, (Dr.) Kříž, Kodíček, Pavel, Srb, Zlámal — but — but
— of course, I earned something on my own, — but mostly my

farcical, scandalous "career" amounted to nothing.* Otherwise, in my opinion all "earned" money stinks absolutely to high heaven, and all social work is an absolute disgrace — a necessary consequence of what I've related from my childhood, of antagonism, of people loathing one another . . . I could see myself living like Robinson Crusoe — or getting my money by stealing, but before I accept any golden handshake on retirement — it's ten times more honest to take gifts from small benefactors. Well, maybe I've even stolen — stealing is the only pure form of purchase among humans.

My whole life has been such a consistent divergence from all that's human, from the very beginning living only for myself, and since I turned 31, only for my Self, that I don't know if anyone could find in all of *history* (leaving aside the long forgotten) such an example. I've always followed a single path — and my life has had a truly singular character. I *couldn't* diverge from it even if I wanted to — the idea of Heracles' crossroads is incomprehensible to me. How small *Heracles* was if mere temptation could blow him over! how small Christ, tempted so modestly! by the devil! One needs to leave such affairs millennia behind. After all, as I've said to myself many times when practical life was getting rough: quit clowning around, live at least for a little while like every other instinctive herd animal, as you lived — most of the time, at least — when you were 7 — for just a little while

* Same goes for my writing. When I was twenty I made myself a rule not to publish anything — unless it was a single, large book when I was old ("pre-Socratic" philosophers — writing became a craft after them). But adverse material conditions forced me to do otherwise.

— I would even try it for a moment (once it even lasted 2 days) to see if it'd work — absurdity of absurdities! as if a hawk wanted to live underwater like a carp! Even if I wanted to, I couldn't, and even if I could, I wouldn't want to . . . "Retreat," says Grabbe's Wellington, "is impossible for two reasons: first of all, our honor would not permit it, and secondly because of the Soignée Forest." But then, it does make me wonder; I have been able to say of myself, since I was 15, the same as Nietzsche: "Ich bin immer am Abgrund." And the idea of sui occisionis is still my sweet companion, reliable as a cane — This has stayed true for 30 years and I'm not the least bit tired of it. — During this time, of course, all my practical affairs have just gone straight to hell — and if I had thought seriously even for a minute of "practical experience," by which here I mean dung, whether it was a career or Napoleonic ambition, it would have been an unprecedented lack of energy on my part. My Superenergy consists of an exemplary lack of what folks call energy. I have enough energy to get myself out of bed at midnight, for no particular reason, as the pecus says, to walk for an hour and a half late at night in the cold just to see what it's like at night around the monument to the heroic Schwerin at Štěrboholy; but until I was 34 I didn't have enough energy to say to someone I met walking: Where does this or that path go? . . . Naturally, I did ask often enough, but I always felt like I was chewing turds. That's characteristic of childhood . . . *That* feeling has grown stronger right up to the present; in part I've become more apathetic, in part more reasonable. Thus far mankind has never known such an Umwertungen der Werte. (My main *service:* a caretaker, slave to the cats . . .)

The fact that I haven't croaked in the last 11 years — and even before that, as I've said, I could have easily, — at any minute (the worst was in 1911, when I was living carefree — I did nothing but stagger around for a couple of months), is for 3 reasons in addition to the above: 1) the art of associating with people; 2) my singularly healthy body, — which not even the most awful, the most "unhealthy" attacks of the mind* could really damage . . . ; and 3) my guardian angel — or "genius," etc. — And also, in fact, in the fourth place, my philosophical fossilization.

Ad primum: I found a modus vivendi with all people — based on a kind of (indulgent) love, stemming from utter contempt — the consequence: in 10 years — although outwardly a rascal dealing with rascals — I had not the least little dispute with people — except for one trifling case when I was in an altogether abnormal and obviously drunk state (immediately after getting soused with methylated spirits). Everyone loves me . . . and I know why —, they are all, without knowing it, metaphysicians — and I am a metaphysician kat' exochen. —

Ad secundum: Emerson says of Napoleon: "Such a body was necessary and such a one was created: a body that could sit 36 (?) hours uninterrupted in the saddle, in the heat and cold, without food, drink, sleep" (quoted loosely). *Napol.* often — if mildly — got sick; me, never; had the flu once, when I was around 12, for about 2 days — I wouldn't have gotten it if I'd been able to

---

* in essence as healthy as the body. But that which is Divine — what is most healthy — must necessarily produce what is most unhealthy in animal existence. Obviously, the human race has seen such cases over and over again. And they have all perished. My Proprietas: the reconciliation of divine and animal energy.

do everything my instincts commanded me at the time: — and since then, nothing! ordinary congestion (even *hay fever*) and toothache don't really count as illness. Once in a while I would try to make myself ill, — doesn't work — unless a person takes cyanide — spending the whole night in the 20-below cold, in a gale, — wearing a summer outfit, — nothing — (by the way: the cold has always bothered me, the worst heat — never; the steamier it is, the easier I find it — like a cat who crawls onto a stove in the worst heat, I'll lie out in the sun when it's 34°C in the shade, happy as a cannibal, and wish: hotter, hotter! Never felt sapped of energy in the worst Central European swelter and when walk-ing record distances). I would glug down bathwater from people with smallpox —, scarf down sausages that were nothing but worms, drink water that would've made a normal person at least seriously ill — I'd just have to contend with two days' diarrhea — Doctors would croak from hunger if all their patients were like me, just like lawyers, bureaucrats, and other offices of that sort, needless for healthy and wise people — of which there are hardly 5 in all of Europe . . . My body's been pretty robust the last 10 years, thanks to my thriftiness: since 1915 I've slept in unheated rooms — dressed any old way, I don't give a damn, health-wise or aesthetically, and 4 crowns is enough for any person for food: eating *only* raw things: it does as much for your wallet as for your health. Cooking is just a waste of time, deprives foods of impor-tant "vitaminous" components, *ruins* their taste and costs two to twenty times as much. — For some time I've eaten only: raw flour (if necessary, wheat or peas soaked in water), raw meat, raw eggs, milk, lemons, and raw vegetables; and my health has been ideal — and no millionaire gourmand ever puked while eating his oysters and other crap like that with as much pleasure as I when tearing into a kilo of raw horse meat . . . To detest something — unknown to me. Once I stole a bitten-into mouse from a cat and gobbled it down, just like it was, with the fur and bones — as if I were eating a dumpling. — I covered 98 km in the Tyrol in 21 hours, and could've kept going for the other 3 hours (of that day) without stopping . . . Etc. — Lots could be said about it — I'm obliged to give thanks to my body, which has always performed wonders as the victim of a reprobate mind. Over the last year, while drinking an awful lot of alcohol, I haven't felt any bodily pains at all — just my shoes pinching. I haven't even had a cold over the last few years. I've never been a soldier, in spite of 7 call-ups, although I'm one of the healthiest people in Austria, and my one physical defect is that although I'm 175 cm tall I've weighed only 62-65 kg. — Whoever believes in mens sana in corpore sano cannot call me a psychopath.

3) My basic rationality, strengthened by the uninterrupted 16-year practice of philosophy. It's taught me to be more forbearing and act more purposefully, without prejudices and emotions and scruples; I consider whatever I do in my practical life to be of no importance, and if I have a hypertrophic social pride, I have a still greater ability to squelch it altogether. *Everything* practical is dishonorable. — My avid, passionate practice of philosophy has not been in vain — True, until I was 40 I told myself that, in this, I'd failed — not having attained, when it was just within reach, the Goal of Goals: eternal, peaceful, invulnerable Joy and Radiance — by not having attained all, I thought, I had attained

nothing. Well, maybe not all, but still *much*. I have just as much right to call myself a philosopher as Xenocrates, Diogenes, Epictetus — And I live in incomparably worse conditions — When I told Böhler that I had simply failed to achieve the Goal, when he answered: "Since the dawn of humanity, who has if not you?!" I laughed at him. But later I understood more and more that in a way he was right. Absoluteness (which I am to the core) scorns all forms of relativism. The Self leads itself to self-depre-cation. — I am nothing other than the steady (often, quite often, in my dreams as well) cracking of the whip of my Absolute Will, commanding absolutely and awash in Itself until the end of time, and the frantic, "irrational," but always more or less obedient whirl of thoughts and mental states, — my life, the greatest buffoonery and quixotism imaginable — because it is at the same time maximally rational, — because I'm still alive, a "moon creature" come to Earth, whose sole activity, not letting up for even a minute, has been persistent laboring against the conditions of animal life. — There is no emotion which would have even a 2% power over me. By nature I'm given to fits of anger — I haven't felt anger for years — apart from swearing when I can't button a collar around my neck; I'm sweetness and mildness personified to all folks. I've almost completely forgotten the sensation of fear — at most I get a whiff of it if I think I'll find an affable guy in the pub who might, out of habit, draw me into conversation. But even before, fear, real fear, was unknown to me; I don't remember ever shaking or going pale from fear — while too often I would turn white with anger. During my late-night walks through deserted places, it never even occurred to me to pay attention if someone was walking toward me or behind me — as a rule I walked right past, and only when I heard the footsteps receding did I sometimes become aware that I had encountered someone; — but it is instructive to watch people, late at night, walking in the fields — as soon as they enter the forest: almost all of them start acting like rabbits — it may be observed here that mankind is made up, on the whole, of total milksops. — I have hardly any desires, aspirations, or appetites, — except for those momentary ones that die as soon as they're born; the same goes for worries. Sorrow, "pangs of conscience," the feeling of guilt, envy, jealousy — have all been unknown to me, for as long as I can remember; they're fitting only for cattle; my sympathy for animals, enormous and awkward, but 90% overcome; for people — almost none; but I am no misanthrope — quite the opposite, I'm fond of people in a special way — as I like lice. If I could destroy all of mankind at one blow — gladly, without anger, just out of "Übermuth"; I wouldn't hesitate to, even for a second — knowing that in All-Being they mean infinitely less than one bacterium does to all the rest of Earth's creatures — and that even All-Being is — Nihil; *that's* what is called knowing how to observe — the *act* of knowing how to observe everything sub specie aeternitatis — of which Masaryk, among others, is so fond — Few people have as many unpleasant emotions as I; but I want them, and they are, if not dear, at least bearable to me. Pleasant ones, *about* the same number, now — before, sometimes, even more — such moments of pure delight, summonable at any time I felt like it, and then growing like an avalanche until I was afraid they would kill me . . . But everything, every little thing is subject to Will alone.

There is no mental state that would not disappear in 3 seconds if I wanted it to. I have become — and am, even in my current highly alcoholic state — a machine. A "mental petrifact" — is what Böhler called me, and I take that as perhaps the greatest compliment I have ever received — in contrast to all modern ways of looking at things.

Ad 4) I would like to prove, on the basis of my own life, that there is a "transcendent deliberateness in All That Happens" (Schopen.) — no less conclusively than any dissertation — *Empirically* — I'm not talking about theoretical proofs. So far this plan has been friendly in dealing with me — it must expect something great from me, otherwise it wouldn't have done so many evidently unnecessary little things (it maliciously leads many people to a certain point and then, like a virtuoso, breaks their neck). It has saved me many times — my having been dazzled — from death's door — in the Alps, my eye on the peak and practically running, I got as far as the edge of an abyss — I know that I couldn't see it, and yet some kind of sudden shock threw me backward — a beautiful feeling: one more step — and 500m downward you fly — . . . I climbed cliffs in the darkest nights — when I looked at them in the daytime, I felt queasy — I wouldn't have wanted to go clambering over them in daylight. And my whole life is like that. Fortuna has smiled on me — and I am proudest of *that* — like Sulla. And by all indications she has other plans for me still. — The passing showers of gloom, now alcohol, for example, do nothing to dampen her favor toward me . . . And it isn't a good idea for anyone to stand in my way . . . There are plenty of examples, starting with the deaths of my relatives — I'm altogether a dangerous person . . . "Unlucky city," says my Argestea, "destined for destruction, innocent — except for its mystical guilt in standing by during the humiliation of the Exalted (the hero Fabio, who was a professor of philosophy there). Woe to him who merely witnessed the great humiliation, twice to him who stood by without acting — thrice to him who came to his aid. It would have been better for him had he never been born . . ."

I could easily end this dream — I've done all that is essential, and a myriad of years has now begun to limp slowly after what I have thought (not written — *which* is peripheral). I have created everything I wanted (within *myself* — which is the essential thing) — but not really. I'm a tree in winter, finished — yet I can still dress myself in leaves, flowers, and fruit — now in this dream (again: mainly for *myself* — only secondarily in literature). By all indications, fate still has something in store for me. It could happen — But without spring there is no verdure. If it's a long time in coming — fine; an early spring isn't good; and he who lives in eternity is not impatient. —

Finis

P.S. Forgot about one very important thing: sex. Except for a few visits to bordellos and encounters late at night in the fields, "nothing serious": not that I wouldn't have liked it, but I didn't have time for it, — just like for my "career." Otherwise, I've consistently given any woman I've met a little pat . . . without ever getting slapped by a one of them or by any husband who happened to notice. I don't even do this because it's pleasant, but because I consider it a matter of good manners and etiquette — instinctively; as my Queen of the Nymphs says: "You uncultured lout, you see 30 beautiful women here and don't have enough sense of honor to pat even one of them on the ass." — Otherwise I intend to enrich sexual "pathology" by discovering about 20 "perversities" unknown until now: that is, erotically I've lived — an awful lot — almost only in fantasies.

written in February 1924

A PRINCE LONGING FOR THE STARS
by Josef Zumr

One needs no lengthy introduction to Ladislav Klíma after hav-ing read "My Autobiography." Given his acute ability to examine himself objectively, it would be difficult to find words that were more authentic than his own. Therefore, I will add here only a few brief comments to provide some context and to point out a few things that Klíma neglects to mention.

Ladislav Klíma was in every way an exceptional individual. He made a deliberate effort to set himself apart from the social con-ventions of his time, both in his opinions and his lifestyle, and that was how he was perceived by his contemporaries. While they understood his exceptional character, they were not prepared to accept his thinking. When he died in 1928 of tuberculosis — the poor man's disease — at the age of forty-nine, Karel Čapek, liberal and democrat, eulogized: "Next to Klíma, Diogenes in his barrel was a homeowner." Indeed, for a third of his life Klíma lived in hotel rooms on the outskirts of Prague where he did not possess even a table. He wrote his essays while lying on the floor. He spurned the amenities of "civilization" on philosophical grounds, not because he was fond of living a bohemian life. As the literary critic Julius Fučík noted: "[Klíma's] death marks the passing of the most outstanding, perhaps we should say the *only* Czech philosopher . . . In a country where pedantic moralists are declared philosophers and chattering journalists poets, he was a pure metaphysical poet whose consciousness embraced the entire world and whose magical words penetrated the depths of the ineffable. In a society where the single idea of a birdbrain suffices to launch a shameless career, he stood absolutely on his independence . . ."

Klíma, in fact, had no desire whatsoever for a career as either an academic philosopher or established writer. A large part of his work, that which he did not destroy, remained in manuscript. So it was that *The Sufferings of Prince Sternenhoch*, his first work of fiction, was not published until just a few weeks after his death. Consequently, he did not live to see the scandal it caused. The publisher had included it in a limited edition of important Czech authors, and a number of schoolmarms who subscribed to the series cancelled in outrage because, as they put it, they did not purchase pornography merely because it had a pretty cover.

It was not until the latter half of the 1920s that Klíma returned to his "romanetto," which is what he called his narrative of Prince Sternenhoch, and gave it its final form. The first version was written between 1906 and 1909, and it was one of thirty novels and a slew of novellas that he wrote during that time. This was a period of creative excess, when after the publication of his first work of philosophy in 1904, *The World as Consciousness and Nothing*, he devoted himself entirely to writing fiction, simply for the pleasure of it and as a break from the mental strain of contemplating deep metaphysical problems.

The Sufferings of Prince Sternenhoch, which Klíma claimed to have "carefully worked out in detail," provides us with valuable insight into his skill as a writer of fiction. Of course the jaded reader of today will hardly be shocked by those scenes that led the schoolmarms to cancel their subscriptions. Compared to the modern horror film, Klíma's horror will hardly disturb our sleep, though episodes in the book rank with those found in Hitchcock and could certainly have served as a model for his films. Indeed a film version was made in 1990 by Jan Němec, entitled *V žáru královské lásky* [In the Flames of Royal Love]. Regardless, there still remains the question of how to categorize the novel.

On first sight it would seem to be a satirical work poking fun at Prussian militarism and the degenerate Junker class, for which Klíma harbored deep contempt. This aspect of the book is certainly in evidence, yet it also bears a striking resemblance to the "gothic" or horror novel. Klíma deliberately tries to evoke powerful emotions and feelings of terror in the reader. Sudden reversals are attended by a mix of motifs both fantastical and rational, and the reader's attention is cleverly engaged by mysterious phenomena. One could believe, if not establish, that Klíma was influenced by Walpole, Lewis, Scott, Hoffmann, and Poe and directly inspired by Lautréamont, in whose wake he found himself in close proximity to the Surrealists. This is suggested by another conspicuous feature of the work: black humor. It is a drastic, sardonic, grotesque humor, the harshness of which is leavened by subtle irony and self-irony. Klíma's place in literary history should properly be located, then, amid all the related currents that flowed into Modernism and that through Surrealism grew into absurdist literature.

Yet these analogies relate to the external aspects of Klíma's work. The author himself gives us a deeper understanding of his intent and the true meaning of all the novel's blackness: "The finale of everything isn't 'nothing' but something more horrible, more incomprehensible, shapeless, monstrous, black — and a celestial refulgence. — I invoke the heart of the world as 'Black Radiance,' 'Black Illusion.'" From this we may conclude that he conceived the novel primarily as *philosophical*, that most important were the ideas he wished to convey.

Klíma greatly enjoyed writing fiction, and he devised several literary techniques that, thanks to other authors, later became part of the collective heritage of twentieth-century prose. Behind all these experiments, however, stood his philosophical thinking, skillfully encoded under a fictional veneer. He does not disown his philosophy, rather, he is of one mind with the dictum of his great paragon, Nietzsche: "I write my works with my entire body and life."

The reader unfamiliar with Klíma's philosophy likely will not suspect that his game of constantly shifting dream and reality, fantasy and reality, illusion and lucidity is not just whim or literary experiment, but the expression of his metaphysical thinking. His is a vision of extreme subjectivism: the world is the creation of the individual's imagination, his plaything; in relation to the world man is a god, is God, directing everything; his will is the highest law, he himself is absolute will. This produces a dialectic of paradoxes. Everything can change into its opposite: truth into lies, lies into truth, logic into illogic; no fixed border exists between dream and reality, life and death. The reader is always left in doubt as to whether Helmut is dreaming or is awake, perceiving reality or suffering from hallucinations, and whether Helga is dead or alive. "At one moment lunacy can seem like reason, at another, reason seems like lunacy," Klíma writes. It is only slightly inconsistent and an obvious concession to literary convention that at the close of the novel the protagonist — who is in essence an ironical and parodic variant of Klíma's god-man longing for the stars — is revealed to have indeed gone mad. All the tempestuous events and horrifying visions have only been the figment of his diseased mind. In Klíma's other work the endings are usually left open, a metaphysical question mark hanging over them — as it did over his life's thought.

Even with all its idiosyncrasies and conceptual difficulty, Klíma's work has gained several generations of appreciative readers in his native country. Despite the fact that publishing his books was prohibited by dictatorial regimes for decades, the rare copy would circulate among readers until it was completely in tatters, and more than one self-sacrificing person took the time to transcribe his work, and in multiple, typewritten copies. His non-conformist attitude, his absurdist vision of the world, and, last but not least, his sense of humor helped people overcome the adversity they faced during those trying times. Numerous artists of all stripes —

novelists, poets, painters, dramatists and musicians — have found in his work a constant source of inspiration, and several philosophers have taken up his thought. Since the 1960s, Klíma's work has also attracted a foreign audience, and *The Sufferings of Prince Sternenhoch* has been published in many European languages.

● ● ●

"Philosophy is the poetry of the intellect," Klíma wrote. His philosophy is certainly not an exact science and it cannot be evaluated as such. His thought has a poetic dimension as well as a lyrical charm. But above all there is his wisdom of life. His paradoxes cast light into the very depths of the soul. "It is necessary to love — to love everything; even that which is most revolting. Love is the cruelest, most difficult thing of all. Herein, however, lies the Mystery: that which is most revolting is more likely to melt into love than that which is only half revolting — —"

"Beauty is love kissing horror."

Prague, June 2000

NOTE ON THE TRANSLATION

If Ladislav Klíma's prose challenges and offends as readily in English as it does in the original Czech, this translation will have hit the mark. Hopefully the novel will also give many readers something to think about and to laugh at.

The Sufferings of Prince Sternenhoch has numerous peculiarities to challenge the translator. The author's vocabulary veers frequently from vulgar to sublime, his thematic material runs from the gutter to high philosophy and (ir)religious parody, and both his spelling and punctuation literally defy convention. I have attempted to preserve as much of the flavor of Klíma's writing as possible, leaving foreign words and phrases in their original languages, translating even his favorite adjectives consistently as often as possible, and respecting the author's syntactical idiosyncracies.

Carleton Bulkin, June 2000

PUBLISHER'S ADDENDUM

For this new edition of *The Sufferings of Prince Sternenhoch* I have consulted Klíma's original handwritten manuscript, which is found in the archives of the Museum of Czech Literature. Where there were discrepancies with the first edition from 1928 — particularly the truncating of obscenities, due no doubt to interwar censorship — these have been emended, as were typographical errors and any instance of infelicitous "interpretation." For "My Autobiography," the 1937 Picka edition was consulted as was the recently published critical edition (in *Mea, Sebrané spisy*, vol. 1, edited with a preface and notes by Erika Abrams [Prague: Torst, 2005]). This was especially valuable in enhancing the notes from our previous edition. Through Abrams's monumental effort the whole of Ladislav Klíma's work is being made available in annotated editions, a boon to scholars, translators, and publishers alike. As of this printing, the volume containing *Utrpení knížete Sternenhocha* has yet to appear.

Prague, 2007

NOTES

THE SUFFERINGS OF PRINCE STERNENHOCH

p. 0   *Sternenhoch:* Stern = star; hoch = high, lofty.

p. 43   *Misera mens humana:* Misery is the human condition.

p. 56   *parcere subjectis et debellare superbos:* Behave humanely toward one's subjects, yet submit the obstreperous to war. Virgil, *The Aeneid* (VI. 853).

p. 61   *tres faciunt collegium:* Three's company. Marcellus, Digesta (50,16,85).

p. 70   *Es braust ein Ruf!:* A cry rings out! First lines of "Die Wacht am Rhein" [The Watch on the Rhein], a patriotic anthem penned in 1840 by Max Scheckenburger and popular in Germany in various wars thereafter.

p. 100 *similia similibus curare:* like cures like.

p. 103 *Podex romanus:* Roman ass.

p. 112 *in rebus psychisis:* in matters of the psyche. The original text has "in rebus psychicis," apparently a misprint.

p. 121 *sit venia verbo:* pardon the expression. Cf. Nietzsche, *The Gay Science*, "Book Three," no. 256.

p. 122 *Heil dir im Siegeskranz:* Hail to you in the victor's laurels.

p. 124 *Dixi!:* I have spoken!

p. 125 *quos ego!:* I'll give it to you! (Neptune threatening the stormy winds.) Virgil, *The Aeneid* (1. 134).

p. 125 *Tua res, Romane, agitur:* Your job, Romans, is to act.

p. 127 *Vicit Caesar:* Victory to Caesar.

p. 128
   And now, my dear little Helmut
   let us be happy and cheerful!
   Let us lie back down
   – e – e – in a soft bed
     (no, better:)
   our sorely tired limbs.
   It's better to fuck in the ass
   than to choke on politics!
   Away with the cares that oppress a Caesar!
   But stop! First I must bring you
   sweet pleasure – – e – e with nice things.
   I want to show you, graciously,
   photographs, – that – belong – to me,
   made in the course of the last three months
   – – e – e by photographing — —
           rats . . .

            (translated by Kevin Blahut)

p. 145 *O tempora, o mores!:* "Oh, the times, oh the morals!" Cicero, *The Catiline Orations* (1. 1). The original text has: "O tempores, o mora!" — apparently a misprint.

p. 161 *efficiens:* cause.

p. 176 *these words, supposedly Zarathustra's:* the quote comes from Nietzsche, *Thus Spoke Zarathustra*, translated by Walter Kaufmann (Modern Library Edition, 1995), p. 41.

p. 184 *Probatum est:* It has been verified, approved.

p. 185 *arteries:* The original edition has "alderie," apparently a printer's error for "arteriae."

p. 186 *Nil desperandum:* Never despair. Horace, *Odes* (1. VII, 27).

p. 189 *Pereat Podex romanus:* Perish, Roman ass.

p. 190 *Wacht am Rhein:* Watch on the Rhein (see note above).

p. 190 *in corpore:* in the flesh.

p. 192 *Deutschland, Deutschland, über Alles:* "Germany, Germany above all," the opening lines to "Das Lied der Deutschen" [The Song of the Germans], Germany's national anthem since 1922.

p. 198 *moriturus:* designated for death; one resolved to die.

MY AUTOBIOGRAPHY

p. 211 *Domažlice:* A town in southwest Bohemia near the border with Bavaria.

p. 211 *Father:* Josef Klíma (1833–1909), trained as a miller, took part in the January Uprising in Poland and then worked as a solicitor in his brother's law office. Well-to-do, he was known to be a fiery orator.

p. 214 *in the space of 8 months:* all died of typhus: Klíma's mother, Josefa, on May 5, 1894; grandmother on June 7, 1894; his mother's sister also in 1894; sister Anděla in February 1895 at the age of ten.

p. 214 *Cisleithania:* the Austrian lands of the Austro-Hungarian Empire.

p. 214 *Modřany:* formerly a village, now a suburb of Prague.

p. 214 *his 24-year-old second wife:* Anna Králíková (1874-1959) married Klíma senior in June 1897.

p. 214 *Eisenstein:* a small town in the Šumava region of southwestern Bohemia, today called Železná Ruda.

p. 215 *Smíchov:* a Prague district. He lived at Plzeňská 40, 3rd floor.

p. 215 *Svět jako vědomí a nic:* Originally published in 1904 at the author's expense, it was reissued by Aventinum in Prague in 1928 with a preface by Klíma a dedicated to M. Bittermann (see note below).

p. 215 *Zbraslav:* a suburb on the southern edge of Prague, previously a village.

p. 215 *Emanuel Chalupný:* (1879-1958), sociologist, lawyer, literary historian, translator, he authored a number of monographs on prominent Czech literary figures and was one of the first to give Klíma's work critical attention.

p. 215 *Vinohrady:* an upscale district of Prague.

p. 216 *Vršovice:* a Prague district. Klíma lived with his father's widow at Na Královce 507.

p. 217 *Horoušánky:* a village near Prague.

p. 217 *Vysočany:* a Prague district. According to Klíma, the Hotel Krása might have been the cheapest in the city.

p. 217 *pučálka:* also a rather old-fashioned word meaning "fried peas."

p. 217 *Antonín Kříž:* (1886-1961) a chemist and later research director at the Škoda factory in Plzeň. One of Klíma's early benefactors.

p. 217 *Franz Böhler:* (1886-1941), a chemist by profession, he met Klíma in 1915 in the Hotel Krása's restaurant and they became fast friends and drinking companions, as well as business partners (short-lived). Together they wrote the novel *Der Gang der blinden Schlange zur Wahrheit.*

p. 217 *caretaker for a small factory:* employment arranged for Klíma by Böhler at a steel spring factory in Prague-Libeň.

p. 218 *ersatz tobacco manufacturer:* many of Klíma's manuscripts are on stationery bearing the company's name: Tabak-Ersatz-Manufaktur. Located on Klimentská Street, Klíma was its sole employee in addition to partner.

p. 218 *Mr. Kodíček:* Josef Kodíček (1892-1954), literary and theater critic; Klíma dedicated *Tractates and Dictates* to him.

p. 218 *the two* Matthews: written with Arnošt Dvořák (see note below), the plays *Matěj Poctivý* [Matthew the Honest], which premiered on February 22, 1922 at Prague's Estates Theater and *Matějovo vidění* [Matthew's Vision], which premiered at the National Theater in November 1923.

p. 218 *Traktáty a diktáty:* (Prague: Otakar Štorch-Marien, 1922). Klíma's preface states that the volume is a collection of essays written for periodicals, all of which save the final two were previously published. The printing was funded by Emanuel Chalupný.

p. 218 *fracturam radius sinistris:* a fracture of the left radius.

p. 219 *Vorsehung:* Providence.

p. 219 *Dr. Dvořák:* Arnošt Dvořák (1881-1933), playwright and theater critic.

p. 219 *intimissimi:* the innermost.

p. 220 *A number of my friends:* those not already mentioned: Maxmilián Bittermann (1890-1973), architect, economist, journalist, he met Klíma in 1913 and in 1925 organized a "relief fund" for him that collected monthly contributions, he himself often paying Klíma's debts at the hotel; Otokar Březina (1868-1929), Symbolist poet, author of *Hidden History*, champion of Klíma's philosophy; Alois Fiedler (1896-1963) met Klíma in 1916 and was generous with his wallet and library as well as keeping him supplied with bread and tobacco until war's end; Antonín Pavel (1887-1958), agronomist, journalist, editor in chief of *Československý deník* [The Czechoslovak Daily], Klíma's third work of philosophy, *Vteřina a věčnost* [A Second and Eternity, 1927] is dedicated to him; Miloš Srb (1892-1944), chemist, industrialist, chamber vocalist, published his own volume of philosophy in 1940; Josef Zlámal (1891-1958) met Klíma in 1922 and many times was his only hope for getting any food.

p. 222 *Ich bin immer am Abgrund:* "I always stand at the edge of the abyss" (cf. *Thus Spoke Zarathustra*).

p. 222 *sui occisionis:* self-destruction, suicide.

p. 222 *pecus:* sheep.

p. 222 *the heroic Schwerin:* Kurt Christoph Graf von Schwerin (1684-1757) was a field marshall under Frederick the Great. He fell at Štěrboholy during the Battle of Prague, at which spot the Austrian authorities erected a monument that stood until after WWII.

p. 222 *Umwertungen der Werte:* transvaluation of values.

p. 223 *art of associating with people:* cf. "The hermit speaks" in Nietzsche, *The Gay Science,* no. 364.

p. 223 *kat' exochen:* preeminent, par excellence.

p. 223 *36 hours in the saddle:* Emerson has "sixteen to seventeen hours."

p. 223 *Proprietas:* speciality, quality, trait.

p. 225 *mens sana in corpore sano:* a sound mind in a sound body. Juvenal, *Satires* (x. 356).

p. 227 *Übermuth:* high spirits, exuberance, hubris.

p. 227 *sub specie aeternitatis:* from the point of view of eternity.

p. 228 *a "transcendent deliberateness in All That Happens":* Klíma's paraphrase of Schopenhauer's essay title "Transcendent Speculation on the Apparent Deliberateness in the Fate of the Individual" in *Parerga and Paralipomena: Six Long Philosophical Essays*, vol. 1 (Oxford: Clarendon Press, 2000).

p. 229 *says my Argestea:* Argestea and Fabio are characters in Klíma's *Velký roman* [Great Novel], *Sebrané spisy*, vol. IV, edited by Erika Abrams (Prague: Torst, 1996). The quote here is a paraphrase of that found on p. 576. Abrams points out that the 1937 Picka edition (and hence subsequent editions based on that) erroneously has "kdo nepomáhal" ("who did not offer aid" in our previous edition) when it should be "kdo napomáhal" ("who came to his aid"). Paradoxical though this may seem, Klíma makes it clear in other versions of this passage that the one who offers help is actually interfering with a higher power.

ABOUT THE CONTRIBUTORS

CARLETON BULKIN received an M.A. in Slavic Languages and Literatures from Indiana University. His translations include *Hidden History* by Otokar Březina (Twisted Spoon Press) and *False Dawn* by Ilona Lacková (University of Hertfordshire Press).

MICHAL VAVREČKA was born in 1975 in Olomouc. He is a graduate of the School of Fine Arts in Prague and now teaches painting at the State Arts School in Český Krumlov.

JOSEF ZUMR is a member of the Philosophy Institute of the Czech Academy of Sciences and teaches philosophy at Palacký University in Olomouc. He has written extensively on Klíma's work.

Ladislav Klíma
The Sufferings
of Prince
Sternenhoch

Translated by Carelton Bulkin
Cover and frontispiece artwork by Michal Vavrečka
Title lettering by Pavel Růt
Typeset in Garamond Semibold
Design by J. Slast

The Sufferings of Prince Sternenhoch originally published in Czech as
Utrpení knížete Sternenhocha – Groteskní romanetto in 1928 by Škeřík, Prague
My Autobiography originally published in Czech as
Vlastní životopis filosofa Ladislava Klímy in 1937 by Jaroslav Picka, Prague

First published in English in hardcover by Twisted Spoon Press in 2000

New edition in paperback 2008

TWISTED SPOON PRESS
P.O. Box 21 – Preslova 12
150 21 Prague 5, Czech Republic
info@twistedspoon.com • www.twistedspoon.com

Printed and bound in the Czech Republic
by PB Tisk, Příbram

Distributed to the trade by

SCB DISTRIBUTORS
15608 South New Century Drive
Gardena, CA 90248-2129, USA
tel: (310) 532-9400, toll free: 1-800-729-6423
info@scbdistributors.com • www.scbdistributors.com

CENTRAL BOOKS
99 Wallis Road
London, E9 5LN, UK
tel: +44 (0)845 458 9911
www.centralbooks.com